THE HEROES

OF TOLKIEN

To my wife, Róisín Magill

Thunder Bay Press
An imprint of Printers Row Publishing Group
9717 Pacific Heights Blvd, San Diego, CA 92121
www.thunderbaybooks.com • mail@thunderbaybooks.com

Correspondence regarding the content of this book should be sent to Thunder Bay Press, Editorial
Department, at the above address. Author and rights inquiries should be addressed to Octopus
Publishing Group Ltd Carmelite House, 50 Victoria Embankment, London EC4Y 0DZ
www.octopusbooks.co.uk

THUNDER BAY PRESS
Publisher: Peter Norton
Associate Publisher: Ana Parker
Publishing/Editorial Team: April Farr, Kelly Larsen, Kathryn C. Dalby
Editorial Team: JoAnn Padgett, Melinda Allman, Traci Douglas, Dan Mansfield

PYRAMID
Publisher: Lucy Pessell
Designer: Lisa Layton
Editor: Sarah Vaughan
Copyeditor: Robert Anderson
Senior Production Manager: Peter Hunt

Illustrations by Mauro Mazzara (cover, 26–27, 46–47, 84–85, 103, 123, 147, 151, 169, 190–191,
251, 220–221, 226–227, 232–233, 234, 238, 247), Andrea Piparo (40–41, 50, 56, 70–71, 126–127,
142–143, 152, 164, 184–185, 200–201, 212, 216–217, 248–249), Allan Curless (75, 91, 133, 134, 162,
172–173), Ian Miller (131, 154, 189, 205), Ivan Allen (15, 19, 37, 61, 89, 98, 115, 139, 179), John
Davis (113, 116, 194), Kip Rasmussen (52, 69, 77, 81, 94), Les Edwards (182), Lidia Postma (141,
174, 180, 222–223), Tim Clarey (230), Victor Ambrus (44–45, 51, 55, 109, 203, 207, 209)

ISBN: 978-1-64517-929-0

Printed in China

26 25 24 23 22   2 3 4 5 6

THE HEROES OF TOLKIEN

DAVID DAY

THUNDER BAY
P · R · E · S · S
San Diego, California

CONTENTS

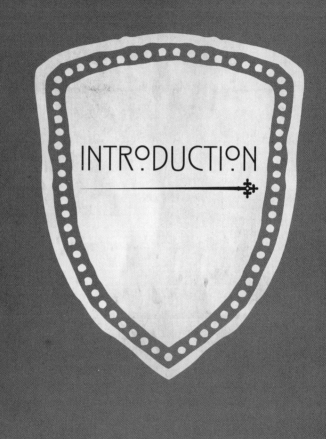

INTRODUCTION

n his famous lecture series *On Heroes, Hero-Worship and the Heroic in History* (1840), Thomas Carlyle proposed the theory that "the history of the world was but the biography of great men." This became known as the "Great Man theory" – the idea that history has been directed and shaped by the will and ambitions of a few "great men" or heroes. It was a theory that enjoyed immense popularity in the Victorian Age, and has found its champions in the twentieth and twenty-first centuries, too.

The history of Tolkien's world is very much shaped by its heroes and heroines. Certainly, in *The Lord of the Rings*, Aragorn the future King of the Reunited Kingdom of Arnor and Gondor is a classic example of a Carlylean hero. By his bravery, strength, ambition and sheer will, Aragorn appears to direct the course of history and bring about the salvation of the Free Peoples of Middle-earth.

However, Tolkien heroes also differ in a number of ways from Carlyle's heroes. Tolkien's heroes are not simply larger-than-life men and women of genius and strength who independently decide the course of history, but are essentially agents of destiny. In Tolkien – as in most fairy-tales and myths – destiny is conveyed or passed on by "a strand of blood". In Tolkien's heroes, their bloodlines are immensely important and may be traced back over thousands of years to semi-divine origins. As we will repeatedly see in this book, the author's heroes and heroines all have rich, deep backstories with frequently complex connections to hereditary ancestors that are ultimately linked to the fates of dynasties and nations.

One cannot entirely understand, for instance, the nature of

Aragorn's destiny or that of his eventual queen Arwen without understanding their ancestry. In *The Heroes of Tolkien*, the commentaries on these two lovers – combined with the "Elven Bloodlines of Aragorn and Arwen Evenstar" chart – trace their royal bloodlines back over seven thousand years of human history – and an additional ten thousand years of Elvish history – to the four original Eldar Kindred, and the High Kings of Eldamar and Beleriand.

Similarly, *The Heroes of Tolkien* is organized in such a manner as to place all of Tolkien's major heroes and heroines – and their ancestors – in their appropriate historical context and chronological order. This has been done to provide readers – particularly those of *The Hobbit* and *The Lord of the Rings* – with insights into the deeper motives for the actions of many of their heroes and heroines, as revealed elsewhere in Tolkien's writings.

Another focus of *The Heroes of Tolkien* is related to how the heroes of Tolkien's world are perceived within the context of world literature, history and mythology. This was a perspective that was immensely important to Tolkien.

The opening essay in Thomas Carlyle's *On Heroes* begins with "The Hero as Divinity" that the term "heroes" should also encompass mythological beings such as Odin and the rest of the Norse gods. Thus, in *The Heroes of Tolkien*, we begin with the divine heroes (and heroines) of Tolkien's world – the Ainur (Valar and Maiar) – comparing them to those same Norse gods (Æsir and Vanir); as well as to that other great pantheon of divine "heroes": the Greco-Roman gods of Olympus.

Thus, although Tolkien's god-like Valar and Maiar are remarkable and original creations, they undoubtedly draw inspiration from the Norse and Greco-Roman gods and goddesses. For example, aspects of Tolkien's Manwë as the king of the Ainur enthroned upon Taniquetil are comparable to those of the Norse Odin as the king of the Æsir enthroned upon Hlidskjalf as well as the Greco-Roman Zeus/Jupiter as the king of the gods enthroned upon Olympus.

Tolkien's intent here was to create a pantheon of archetypal divine and earthly heroes that would place his cosmology of Middle-earth and the Undying Lands on equal footing with authentic mythological traditions of other nations. It was Tolkien's belief that aside from *Beowulf* and a few surviving fragments of poems, the English (Anglo-Saxons) "had no stories of their own, not of the quality that I sought, and found in the legends of other lands".

For beyond his wish to just tell very good stories, Tolkien's greatest ambition was to create a mythology for England. "I had in mind to make a body of more or less connected legend, ranging from the large and cosmogenic, to the level of romantic fairy-story … which I could dedicate simply: to England; my country."

Consequently, in *The Heroes of Tolkien*, the reader will discover that the High Elven hero Fëanor as the creator of the Silmarils was linked in Tolkien's mind to the supernatural smith, Ilmarinen, as the creator of the Sampo in the Finnish epic, *The Kalavala*. Likewise, in the Noldor King Fingolfin, we may recognize elements of the Dagda, the Irish King of the immortal Tuatha Dé Danann.

Certainly, as Tolkien himself acknowledged, the tale of the star-crossed lovers Beren and Lúthien in *The Silmarillion* was inspired by the ancient Greek myth of Orpheus and Eurydice. And Tolkien's dragon-slayer, Túrin Turambar, in many aspects of his life and adventures is comparable to the Norse dragon-slayer Sigurd, the hero of the *Völsunga* saga.

Then too, the lives of Tolkien's Peredhil (half-elven twins): the immortal Elrond and mortal Elros were in part inspired by the Greek Dioscuri (divine twins): the immortal Castor and the mortal Pollux. While another pair of brothers, Isildur and Anárion, as the founders of Gondor, are comparable to the brothers Romulus and Remus, as the founders of Rome.

In *The Lord of the Rings*, we have many elements of the Arthurian theme of the "return of the king" embodied in the actions of the heroes Aragorn and Gandalf that are foreshadowed in the tales of King Arthur and his mentor Merlin the Wizard.

Other heroes and heroines were inspired on the lesser "level of romantic fairy tales". As readers of *The Heroes of Tolkien* may be surprised to discover, the origin of Dwarf King Durin the Deathless, along with Tolkien's three greatest queens – Arwen Undómiel, Galadriel of Lórien and Varda Elentári – may be discovered in the fairy tale of "Snow White and the Seven Dwarves".

Still other heroes were inspired by historic figures. King Théoden of Rohan was in large part inspired by the historic fifth-century-BCE King Theodoric the Goth; while King Helm Hammerhand (builder of Helm's Dike) can be linked to the historic Offa of Mercia (builder of Offa's Dike). And certainly, Tolkien himself observed that Aragorn's rise to High King of the Reunited Kingdom was comparable to that of

Charlemagne's rise to Emperor of the Holy Roman Empire.

It is interesting to observe that in *The Silmarillion* and the annals of Middle-earth and the Undying Lands before the appearance of the Hobbits in the second half of the Third Age, Tolkien's heroes were largely in tune with the Carlylean ideal – the "great men". However, by the time of the Quest of the Lonely Mountain and the War of the Ring, the real agents of destiny were not always the most obvious of heroes.

Although there is a bounty of heroes in the classic mode in *The Hobbit* and *The Lord of the Rings*, the real agents of destiny were not all to be discovered among those usually considered "the good and the great". As Tolkien observed in his fiction, as in life, courage was often to be found in the most "unlikely places".

In *The Hobbit*, it is the "original" Hobbit, Bilbo Baggins, who becomes the reluctant hero, triggering the events that end the terror of Smaug the Golden Dragon. In *The Lord of the Rings*, the destruction of Isengard by the Ents is the result of the interventions of Meriadoc Brandybuck and Peregrin Took. It is Merry Brandybuck, again, who plays an essential role in the slaying of the Witch-king, and Samwise Gamgee who mortally wounds Shelob the Great Spider. And, ultimately, it is the humble Frodo Baggins – not the mighty, "conventional" hero Aragorn – who stands on the edge of the Cracks of Doom and brings the War of the Ring to its cataclysmic end.

Just as Tolkien's vision of heroes is finally broader than Carlyle's, so is his vision of heroism itself. Tolkien's personal perspective on heroism can be deduced from his observation that (though he could not claim his bravery) the character in *The Lord of the Rings* he most resembled was Faramir, the Captain of Gondor. So, if we see Faramir as a cypher for the author, Tolkien's opinion might best be summed up in that particular hero's eloquent statement: "I do not love the bright sword for its sharpness, not the arrow for its swiftness, nor the warrior for his glory. I love only for that which they defend."

As with all the books in this series, *The Heroes of Tolkien* is written and illustrated in a way that is both informative and accessible to the general reader. All the illustrations, charts and commentaries in *The Heroes of Tolkien* are meant as guides and aids to the reading and comprehension of Tolkien's works. These are handbooks that attempt to give new and entertaining perspectives on Tolkien's world, but are, of course, no substitute for the reading of the works themselves.

Yavanna Kementári

PART

ONE

HEROES OF THE VALARIAN AGES: THE VALAR AND MAIAR

IN THE BEGINNING

I n J. R. R. Tolkien's tale of the creation of Arda (the world), the Ainulindalë, included as the first part of *The Silmarillion*, we can see biblical language and themes that add undeniable grandeur to the events. In this creation tale we also see that, behind the multiplicity of appearances, Tolkien's conception was of a single divine entity, not far removed from the Judeo-Christian god, the Hebrew Yahweh (often Latinized as Jehovah in the English-speaking world).

Tolkien's Eru "the One" – known to the Elves as Ilúvatar, "the Father of All" – is certainly comparable to Yahweh/Jehovah. In the beginning, Tolkien tells us, Eru Ilúvatar's "thoughts" took the form of entities known as the Ainur, "Holy Ones". These vastly powerful spirits are comparable to Judeo-Christian angels and archangels. In the Timeless Halls before the creation of the world, Ilúvatar commanded the Ainur to sing in a celestial choir. And, we are told, this angelic music revealed Eru Ilúvatar's vision of "what was, and is, and is to come".

The contribution of the Judeo-Christian tradition to Tolkien's imaginative writing is profound in its moral implications. However, in most other respects, the early Judeo-Christian world is very unlike Tolkien's. For, although the inhabitants of Tolkien's world do not quite worship "gods", their beliefs are very much closer to the pantheism of the ancient Greeks, Romans and Germanic peoples than they are to the fierce monotheism of the ancient Israelites.

Eru the One

THE "POWERS OF ARDA" AND THE CLASSICAL PANTHEON

In the second part of *The Silmarillion*, known as the Valaquenta, the early history of the heroic lives of the great and the good among the Ainur is revealed in the wake of their entry into the dimensions of time and space and their taking on of physical forms in the newly created world of Arda. These newly transformed entities were made up of two orders – the Valar and the Maiar. These, as Tolkien fully acknowledged, strongly resemble the gods and demigods of pagan European mythology, most especially those of ancient Greece and Rome.

The Valar and Maiar are the ruling "Powers of Arda", and, in describing their arrival, Tolkien attempted to lay the foundations for an entire mythological system. His hope was that this system, which he described as "ranging from the large and cosmegonic, to the level of romantic fairy-story", would be convincing enough to be comparable to the mythological traditions and literatures of European nations.

Tolkien left somewhat conflicting estimates of the period of time during which the Valar and Maiar were the sole or primary occupiers of Arda, but certainly the span between the creation of Arda and the awakening of the Firstborn race of the Elves was not less than twenty thousand years, as humans now measure time. These Valarian Ages saw the Valar and Maiar work tirelessly to shape the physical world of Arda and to bring forth and nurture many new life forms.

The king of the Valar is Manwë, the Lord of the Air, who rules from his throne and palace (Ilmarin) on the top of Taniquetil, the tallest mountain in the world. Manwë is very like Zeus – whom the Romans equated with Jupiter – the king of the gods who ruled from his throne and palace on the top of Mount Olympus, the tallest mountain known to the early Greeks. The eagle was sacred to Zeus, as it is to Manwë, and both are fierce, bearded storm gods.

Manwë's mightiest brothers, Ulmo, the Lord of the Waters of Arda, and Mandos, the Lord of the Halls of Mandos (or Awaiting), had direct counterparts in Greco-Roman mythology. Ulmo shares most of his attributes with Poseidon, the mighty Greek god of the sea, whom the Romans knew as Neptune. Both take the form of giant, bearded ocean lords who are also masters of earthquakes and ride foaming horse-drawn chariots on the crests of tidal waves.

Mandos, the Doomsman of the Valar – who is also known as Namo – shares many characteristics with Hades, the Greek god of the Underworld, whom the Romans knew as Pluto. Both ruled over a place in which the dead or awaiting spirits abided in a confined kingdom, and both had foreknowledge of the fate of mortals and immortals alike.

Among the Valarian goddesses, Yavanna, who is the queen of all growing things, and her younger sister, Vána, who is the queen of the blossoming flowers, have direct parallels in the Greco-Roman pantheon. The Greek goddess of the harvest and agriculture is Demeter (the Roman Ceres) while her daughter is the goddess of the spring, Persephone (the Roman Proserpina).

Varda Elentári, as spouse to Manwë, is primarily comparable to the Greek goddess Hera, wife of Zeus (the Roman Juno) because of their rank as queens. However, they are dissimilar in that Hera is the goddess of marriage and family, while Varda is the Vala of starlight; Hera is jealous and vengeful while Varda is loving and merciful. In this respect, she actually shares more attributes with Asteria, the Greek deity of the stars.

In Tolkien's Valarian god Aulë the Smith, we have a counterpart to the Greek Hephaestus and the Roman Vulcan. Both are capable of forging untold wonders from the metals and elements of the Earth. Both are armourers and jewellers to the gods. Other Valar comparable to Greco-Roman gods are Tulkas the Strong, who shares many characteristics with the Greek strongman Heracles (the Roman Hercules), and Oromë the Hunter, who bears a partial resemblance to the Greek hero and huntsman Orion.

THE NORSE DIMENSION

A lthough the influence of the Greco-Roman gods is most obvious in terms of the hierarchical structure and attributes of Tolkien's Valarian pantheon, in appearance and temperament the Valar and Maiar have far more in common with the gods of northern Europe – of the Norsemen and other Germanic peoples.

A wild and dark sense of doom pervades Norse mythology, making it seem far removed from the sunlit Mediterranean world of the Greek and Roman gods, among whom, despite their fits of jealousy and rage, reigns a certain spirit of wisdom and reason. By contrast, the heroes of Norse myth and most of the heroes of Tolkien's tales share a philosophy of stoic fatalism and a stubborn code of personal honour that (usually) encourages the pursuit of a fearless warrior's death. Both the Norse heroes and Tolkien's heroes await a doom wherein a supreme cataclysm will end the world. This is the great conflict of elemental forces that the Vikings called Ragnarök and Tolkien called the World's End.

Tolkien's vision of the World's End is deliberately veiled, but there are clear similarities between the Viking Ragnarök and Tolkien's cataclysmic Great Battle in the War of Wrath. Ragnarök will be a battle between the gods and the giants and will commence when Heimdall, the watchmen of the gods, blows his horn. Similarly, Tolkien's disastrous Great Battle begins with a trumpet blast from Eönwë, the Herald of the Valar.

Tolkien's inspiration is drawn from a far wider range of sources than a brief comparison of cosmologies might suggest. However, the influence of Norse myth in the shaping of Tolkien's world is deep and undeniable. One might begin by looking at the complex nature of the king of the Norse gods and comparing him to Tolkien's Manwë, the king of the Valar.

Manwë, the Lord of the Air, is, of course, far more obviously similar to the Olympian Zeus. However, he does share some of the characteristics of the Norse King of the Gods in his guise as Valdr Vagnbrautar, "Ruler of Heaven". Both Manwë and Odin are stern, grey-bearded and of gigantic size, and both wear blue-mantled cloaks. Both are considered the wisest and most terrifying of the gods. Manwë, the king of the Valar and Maiar, is enthroned on Taniquetil, the highest mountain in the world, from where his all-seeing eyes can survey the entire world. Odin, as king of the Æsir, is enthroned on Hlidskjalf, the Watchtower of the Gods in Asgard, where his single all-seeing eye can stare out over all the Nine Worlds.

In Njord, the Norse god of the sea, we have a reasonable match with Tolkien's Ulmo, the Lord of Waters, whose rise from the deep is announced by the sounding of the Ulumúri, his great conch-shell horn. Among the Maiar sea spirits who serve Ulmo are Ossë of the Waves and his spouse, Uinen of the Calms. These two had counterparts in the lesser Norse sea god Ægir and the sea goddess Rán.

There are some general comparisons between Varda Elentári, spouse of Manwë, and the Norse spouse of Odin, the Æsir goddess Frigg, who was frequently identified with the Vanir goddess Freya, the spouse of Odin. But neither of these is a sky deity like Varda, whose epithet Elentári means "Star Queen" in Quenya.

Nor did Norse mythology really have a smith god comparable to Tolkien's Aulë, whom the Dwarves call Mahal "the Maker" as it was he who conceived their race. However, Norse myths do have the Dwarf smith Brokkr who was called upon to forge the weapons and jewels of the gods. In addition, there is another legendary mortal king and hero named Völundr who was also known as Wayland the Smith.

The realms of the dead in Tolkien's tales and Norse myths are as different from one another as are their rulers. Mandos the Doomsman was the stern but benign Lord of the Halls of Awaiting while the Norse ruler of the misty underworld of

Next page: Ulmo, Lord of Waters

Niflheim was Hel, a frightening goddess whose subjects were those who died of sickness and disease.

The Valarian hero Tulkas the Strong has a partial counterpart in the Norse god Magni the Strong, the son of Thor, the thunder god. Then there is Oromë, the Huntsman of the Valar, who rides like the wind through the forests of Arda while blowing his hunting horn, the Valaróma. Oromë was almost certainly partly inspired by the terrifying Woden or Wotan, Lord of the Wild Hunt, another guise of the great god Odin.

Certainly, aspects of Yavanna, the Valarian guardian of growing things, can be related to Sif of the Golden Hair, the Norse goddess of the harvest. Similarly, Yavanna's sister and Oromë's spouse, the beautiful Vána the Ever-young, a spirit who delights in spring flowers and the birds of the forest, appears to be adapted from a combination of the spring goddess Eostre and Idunn, the Norse goddess of eternal youth.

In the Valarian Estë the Gentle and the Norse Eir the Merciful we have comparable goddesses of healing, while in Tolkien's Nienna the Weeper and the Norse Hlin the Shelterer we discover

Yavanna Kementári

complementary goddesses of mourning, grief and consolation. In the Valarian lord Lórien we have a master of dreams, and in the Norse goddess Nott, the personification of night, we also have a mistress of dreams. And in Tolkien's Vairë the Weaver and the Norse Urd, we have a pair of spirits who govern destiny.

Among the Maiar spirits we also discover personifications of the Sun and Moon like those found in Norse mythology. The Norse personification of the Sun is the female Sunn, comparable to the female Maia spirit of fire, Arien the Golden, guardian of the Sun; while the Norse personification of the Moon is the male Máni, comparable to the male Maia Tilion of the Silver Bow, guardian of the Moon. It is worth noting that the ancient Greeks gendered the celestial bodies the other way round to both the Norse and Tolkien, venerating the sun god Helios and the moon goddess Selene.

Aulë Mahal

Arien the Sun and Tilion the Moon

HEROES AND VILLAINS

n this brief review of the Valar and Maiar, we have naturally
enough focused on the "heroes", not the anti-heroes and
outright villains of the Tolkienian world. However, it is
worth drawing attention here to the figure of Melkor/Morgoth
– the fallen Vala. For this Satan-like figure, Tolkien again drew
inspiration from the Norse god Odin, not in his more benign
guise as Ruler of Heaven but as the Sorcerer King.

In Odin, we find one of the most complex and ambivalent

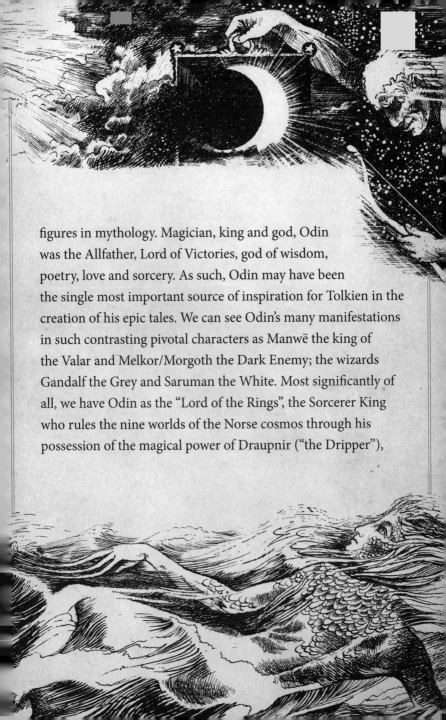

figures in mythology. Magician, king and god, Odin was the Allfather, Lord of Victories, god of wisdom, poetry, love and sorcery. As such, Odin may have been the single most important source of inspiration for Tolkien in the creation of his epic tales. We can see Odin's many manifestations in such contrasting pivotal characters as Manwë the king of the Valar and Melkor/Morgoth the Dark Enemy; the wizards Gandalf the Grey and Saruman the White. Most significantly of all, we have Odin as the "Lord of the Rings", the Sorcerer King who rules the nine worlds of the Norse cosmos through his possession of the magical power of Draupnir ("the Dripper"), a gold ring that shed eight more gold rings every nine days.

Although there are many links between Tolkien's world and the legends and myths of many other nations and civilizations, we should never lose sight of the fact that the genius of the author lay in his ability to integrate all those elements into a single, self-contained mythological system. Without that remarkable integrating power of his imagination, there would have been no creative spark to bring his characters to life, leaving a world that would appear an unconvincing assemblage of mythic themes and allusions. As it is, Tolkien succeeded magnificently in his desire to create a body of work that could be favourably compared to the mythological traditions and literatures of nations.

MAIA	GRECO-ROMAN GOD	NORSE GOD
Eönwë Herald of Manwë	Hermes/Mercury	Heimdall Watchman of the Æsir
Ilmarë Handmaid of Varda	Asteria/Virgo	Berchta the Bright
Arien The Sun	Helios/Sol	Sunn The Sun
Tilion The Moon	Selena/Luna	Mani The Moon
Ossë Maia of the waves	Pontus/Pontus	Aegir Sea God
Uinen Maia of the calms	Thalassa/Thalassa	Rán Sea Goddess

VALA	GRECO-ROMAN GOD	NORSE GOD
Manwë Sulimo	Zeus/Jupiter	Odin Valdr
Lord of the Air	Lord of the Skies	King of Asgard
Varda Elentári	Hera/Juno	Frigg/Freya
Lady of the Stars	Queen of the Gods	Queen of the Æsir/Vanir
Ulmo	Poseidon/Neptune	Njord
Lord of Waters	God of the Seas	Vanir God of the Seas
Yavanna Kementári	Demeter/Ceres	Sif of the Golden Hair
Queen of the Earth	Goddess of the Earth	Goddess of the Harvest
Vána the Ever-young	Persephone/Proserpina	Eostre/Idunn the Youthful
Vala of Spring	Goddess of Spring	Goddess of Spring and Youth
Aulë Mahal	Hephaestus/Vulcan	Volundr/Wayland
Smith of the Valar	Smith of the Gods	Smith to the Gods
Mandos Namo	Hades/Pluto	Hel of Niflheim
Lord of the Underworld	God of Underworld	Goddess of the Underworld
Tulkas Astaldo	Heracles/Hercules	Magni the Strong
Strongest of the Valar	Strongest of Gods	Strongest of the Æsir
Oromë Tauron	Orion/Orion	Woden/Wotan
The Huntsman	The Hunter	Lord of the Wild Hunt
Nessa the Swift	Artemis/Diana	Holda/Holle
Vala of the Forests	Goddess of the Forests	Goddess of the Forest
Lórien Irmo	Morpheus/Somnia	Nott/Night
Master of Dreams	God of Dreams	Goddess of Dreams
Estë the Gentle	Hygeia/Hygia	Eir the Merciful
Vala of Healing	Goddess of Healing	Goddess of Healing
Nienna the Weeper	Penthos /Luctus	Hlin the Shelterer
Vala of Grief and Mourning	God of Grief and Mourning	Goddess of Mourning
Vairë the Weaver	Clotho/Nona	Urd the Weaver
Weaver of Fates	Morae/Parcae Weaver of Fates	Norn Weaver of Fates

PART
TWO.

HEROES OF
THE AGES OF
STARS: ELDAR
AND SINDAR

THE ELDAR OF ELDAMAR

escribing the creation of his Elves, Men and Dwarves, Tolkien speaks of "awakenings", implying that each race existed in some sense prior to their arrival in Middle-earth, as conceptual rather than physical beings. The Elves are from the moment of their awakening associated with starlight. In the same hour that Varda Elentári, the Queen of the Heavens, sets the stars ablaze in the dark skies above Middle-earth, the Elves – the First Children of Eru Ilúvatar – awake by the mere of Cuiviénen, the "Waters of Awakening". This marks the beginning of the First Age and the heroic age of the Elves.

The first named in this history is Ingwë, the high king of the Elves, who might best be described as the Moses of the Elves. For, just as Moses in the Hebrew Bible was chosen by God to lead the Hebrews out of Egypt to their Promised Land, so Ingwë was chosen by the Valar to lead the first of the Elves in the Great Journey out of Middle-earth to their promised land of Eldamar ("Elvenhome").

Ingwë was the lord of the First Kindred of the Elves, known as the Vanyar, or the "Fair Elves". We know exactly what the philological sources for Ingwë are, as Tolkien once wrote of a Northern heroic warrior named Ingeld, the son of Froda, who was prince of the Heathobards and enemy of the Shield-Danes of

Beowulf. Tolkien discovered that behind this tale was a "god of the Angles called Ing".

Tolkien's Elven high king Ingwë, like the biblical Moses, leads his people to a "promised land", in *The Silmarillion* the Undying Lands. Whereas Moses dies on Mount Nebo, just before reaching the Promised Land, Ingwë accompanies his people to the very end of their journey. On the hill of Túna in Eldamar, Tolkien tells us, Ingwë raised the white towers and crystal stairs of the city of Tirion and ruled there for a time as high king of the Eldar. Later, however, he departed with the greater part of the Vanyar and finally settled on the slopes of Mount Taniquetil where stood the Halls of Manwë Súlimo, king of the Valar.

Finwë was the lord of the Second Kindred of the Elves, the

The westward migration of the Elves

Noldor, who undertook the Great Journey over the wilds of Middle-earth and into the Undying Lands of the Valar. In the High Elvish language of Quenya, "noldor" means "knowledge". We now know from Tolkien's original drafts that these Elves were originally to be called the "Gnomes" (derived from the Greek "gnosis", also meaning "knowledge").

Very quickly in *The Silmarillion* it is the Noldor who become the focus of most of Tolkien's heroic tales, often achieving a tragic grandeur due to their passions and flaws, much like the characters from Greek tragedy or the Norse sagas. The Noldor, Tolkien relates, were the greatest craftsmen of the Elves in the shaping of jewels and forging of metals. On settling in the immortal land of Eldamar, they became apprentices to Aulë the Smith – who here as mentor to the Elves takes on a similar role to the Greek Prometheus, who gives men the gift of fire and the basics of civilization. From Aulë the Noldor learned all the secrets of the treasures to be found deep within the Earth. For their knowledge and skill, the Noldor (as the meaning of the name in the Quenya tongue suggests) became known as the "Wise Elves" and the "Deep Elves".

The Third Kindred of the Eldar was led into the Undying Lands by King Olwë. These were the Teleri, or "those who come last". Tolkien's classification of the Elves in terms of "kindreds" appears to come from the Welsh faerie spirits known as the Tylwyth Teg, or "beautiful kindred". The Teleri were the most numerous of the three kindreds and so loved the sea and the stars that they wished to settle on the starlit shores of Eldamar. On Tol Eressëa, the "Lonely Isle", in the Bay of Eldamar, Olwë founded Avallónë as the island's principal port and city. Soon other cities prospered on the island, and Olwë – known for his long white hair and blue eyes – eventually explored the north coast where he founded the greatest city of the Teleri – Alqualondë, the Haven of Swans.

In Avallónë, we see a typical literary Tolkien device by which he claims to discover the "true" origin of a real-life legend within his fictional Elven histories. In this case, Avallónë is seen to prefigure the island and earthly paradise of Avalon, where the mortally wounded King Arthur was healed by the nine queens of Avalon. Avalon means "Isle of Apples" and can be related to the Garden of the Hesperides in Greek mythology, where the beautiful daughters of Atlas and Hesperis ("West Wind") tend the tree that bears the golden apples of immortality. Memories and dreams of the Valarian Trees of Light in the Undying Lands, Tolkien would have us believe, inspired many stories of western isles and lands where trees bore "Golden Apples of the Sun" and "Silver Apples of the Moon".

Next page: The city of Tirion in Eldamar

THE GREAT JOURNEY

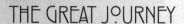

Tolkien's Great Journey of the Elves was in large part his means of giving definition to the Elves from a multitude of lost traditions and mythologies that had been reduced by the passage of history to descriptions of a single word: light, dark, green, grey, sea, sylvan, river or wood. Tolkien came to the rescue of these long-lost nations and brought them to life again in the pages of literature. In writing *The Silmarillion*, Tolkien gave life and context to the long histories of more than 40 kindreds, ethnicities and city-states of Elves.

Tolkien insisted on clarifying definitions by making "Elfin" become "Elven". He wished to define the "Elves" as a distinct and singularly important "species". In many languages, the word "elf" is associated with the colour white (for example, the Latin *alba* and Greek *alphos* both mean "white"), and the word also retains an association with "swan". Britain was once known as Albion, a name that Tolkien implies can be literally translated as "Elf-land".

In Norse mythology, there are references to the "Light Elves" of Alfheim (meaning "Elf Home") and the rather sinister "Dark Elves" of the subterranean Svartalfheim ("Black Elf Home"). The latter were rehabilitated by Tolkien and their existence explained by the "sundering" of the Elves during the Great

Journey. Tolkien's Calaquendi ("Light Elves") were the Eldar, the High Elves of Eldamar who made the journey to Eldamar ("Elvenhome"). Tolkien's Moriquendi ("Dark Elves") were the Avari, or Refusers, those who remained under the starlight in the east of Middle-earth and never saw the divine Trees of Light in the Undying Lands.

In the Great Journey of the Elves, Tolkien also set out to link the Elves with the mythology of the ancient Celts. To this end, Tolkien's account of the discovery of the Elves in the east of Middle-earth by Oromë, the Huntsman of the Valar, who befriends and guides them to a land of immortals, was inspired by legends of a similar figure among the ancient Britons. The Welsh Arawn was an immortal huntsman who, like Oromë, rode like the wind through the forests of the mortal world. Arawn befriended a mortal Welsh king and acted as his guide into the Otherworld of Annwn. The parallel is strengthened by the fact that Oromë was known to the Sindar as Araw the Huntsman.

Tolkien's Elves are largely based on the Celtic myths, legends and traditions of Ireland and Wales. We might even go so far as to state that the Elves themselves have Celtic characteristics, while his Men have characteristics of the invading Anglo-Saxons, who pushed the Britons and their culture to the margins of the British Isles.

It is important to understand that, before Tolkien, the "Elf" was – at least in modern times – a vaguely defined concept associated most often with pixies, flower-fairies, gnomes, dwarfs and goblins of a diminutive and inconsequential nature. Tolkien's Elves are not a race of pixies. They are a powerful, full-blooded people who closely resemble the pre-human Irish race of immortals called the Tuatha Dé Danann. Like the Tuatha Dé Danann, Tolkien's Elves are taller and stronger than mortals, are incapable of suffering sickness, are possessed of more than human beauty, and are filled with great wisdom in all things. They possess talismans, jewels and weapons that humans might consider magical. They

Ingwe leads Vanyar in the Great Journey

ride supernatural horses and understand the languages of animals. They love song, poetry and music – all of which they compose and perform perfectly.

❦

Next page: Olwë of the Teleri

THE TUATHA DÉ DANANN

The Tuatha Dé Danann gradually withdrew from Ireland as mortal men migrated there from the east. In his ever-present theme of the dwindling of Elven power in Middle-earth, Tolkien was following the tradition of Celtic myth and history. The Elves' westward sailings to timeless immortal realms across the sea, leaving Men to assert their dominance in the mortal, diminished world of Middle-earth, very much reflect the diminishing of the Tuatha Dé Danann.

Both the Elves and the Tuatha Dé Danann are immortal in the sense that their lifespan is unlimited, though they can be killed. Tolkien follows the Celtic tradition that suggests that immortals cannot survive in the mortal world and can remain only at the cost of the loss of their powers. Ultimately, there is a choice between remaining in the mortal world and leaving it forever for an immortal, timeless world in a dimension beyond the reach of human understanding.

Although Tolkien used elements of Celtic myth in the creation of his Elves, his own contribution to these creatures of his imagination is immense and remarkable. Tolkien took the sketchy myths and legends of the Tuatha Dé Danann and created a vast Elvish civilization, history and genealogy. This vast cultural treasure trove may have been rooted in real myths and legends but only really bloomed and flourished through the workings of the writer's imagination.

THE SINDAR, OR GREY ELVES

Beyond his distinction between Elves of Darkness (those who never saw the light of Valinor) and Elves of the Light (those who did), Tolkien also created a new category of Elves – a kind of twilight people known as the Sindar, or Grey Elves. At the beginning of the Great Journey, the first lord of the Teleri in their westward migration was not Olwë, but his elder brother, Elwë. However, in Beleriand in the north-west of Middle-earth, Elwë abandoned the Great Journey, having come under the spell of the Maia Melian, a beautiful spirit who had once tended the flowering trees in the Dreamland of Lórien in Valinor and who now dwelt in the forests of Beleriand.

Tolkien's Elves are often as closely related to forests as they are to the stars. In Tolkien's earliest drafts of *The Silmarillion*, his original name for Beleriand was Broceland. This name was seemingly inspired by the forest of Brocéliande found in medieval Arthurian romances, itself based on an actual forest in Brittany. Tolkien's Beleriand – and Elwë's kingdom of Doriath in particular – was to a considerable degree modelled on Brocéliande, a vast forest realm with magical fountains, glittering

Elwë's hidden Sindarin city of Menegroth

grottos and hidden palaces, all protected by the powerful spell of an enchantress.

Tolkien explains that when Elwë returned from the forest of Nan Elmoth his hair had turned silver and he had shining eyes, whereupon his name was changed to Thingol, meaning "Greymantle". By this time most of the Teleri, despairing of Elwë's return, had already left for Eldamar. Those who stayed behind were given the name of Sindar, or "Grey Elves", suggestive of their in-between, twilight status, neither dark nor light. King Thingol and his queen, Melian, found a kingdom in Nan Elmoth, known as Doriath, with the glittering mansions of the "Thousand Caves" of Menegroth as its citadel.

The Arthurian tales of Brocéliande and its enchantments were often somewhat less benign in nature, though like Doriath its "magic" was feared. The best known of its enchantresses was Vivien, the Lady of the Lake. The most famous legend tells how Vivien came upon Merlin asleep beneath a thorn tree in the forest and ensorcelled the magician in a "tower of air" from which he could never emerge. Vivien's spell rendered him invisible, but to this day, it is claimed, the faint and distant voice of the magician may be heard in the forest bewailing his fate.

The enchanted, perhaps perilous forest realm is a motif that returns repeatedly in Tolkien's works – in the kingdom of Thranduil in Mirkwood and Galadriel's domain, Lothlórien, in the shadow of the Misty Mountains. The prototype, however, is Doriath, where King Thingol, as high king of the Elves of Beleriand, rules through thousands of years of peace and prosperity. During this time Melian gives birth to the only child of Eldar and Maia blood, the incomparably beautiful Princess Lúthien, one of the key figures in the heroic tales of *The Silmarillion*.

*Elwë, Melian and Lúthien –
Rulers of Sindaran
Grey Elves*

THE SINDARIN LANGUAGE OF THE GREY ELVES

T he language of the Eldar of Eldamar was Quenya, from the root word *quendi*, meaning the "speakers" as the Elves were the first race to develop a spoken language – and later also devised a written language. However, it was the language of the Grey Elves, Sindarin, that became the common tongue of the Elves in the western lands of Middle-earth.

The degree to which Tolkien's Elves were inspired by Celtic models is most obviously demonstrated by looking at his invented Grey Elf language, Sindarin. Tolkien himself noted that Sindarin names for persons, places and things were "mainly deliberately modelled on those of Welsh (closely similar but not identical)". Structurally and phonetically, there are strong links between the two languages.

A few words are identical: *mal* means "gold" in both the Welsh and Sindar tongues. Others are close: *du* means "black" in Welsh and "shadow" in Sindarin; *cal an* means "first day" in Welsh and "daylight" in Sindarin; *ost* means "host" in Welsh and "town" in Sindarin; *sam* in Welsh means a "stone causeway" and in Sindarin a "stone in a ford". There are many others close in spelling and meaning: "fortress" is *cacr* in Welsh and *caras* in Sindarin; *drud* in Welsh means "fierce" while *dru* in Sindarin

Opposite: Melian and Thingol

means "wild"; *dagr* in Welsh means "dagger" while *dagor* in Sindarin means "battle". Others are the same words with different meanings: *adan* is "birds" in Welsh and "man" in Sindarin; *ucu* is "heaven" in Welsh and "water" in Sindarin; *nar* is "lord" in Welsh and "sun" in Sindarin. Some others are strangely connected: *iar* in Sindarin means "old", while the Welsh *iar* means "hen"; however, the Welsh word *hen* actually means "old". With this in mind, Tolkien took the names of a few of his characters directly from Welsh words: Morwen can be related to the Welsh for "maid"; Bard means "poet"; Barahir means "long-beard".

FORGING THE SILMARILS

T he creator of the three gems known as the Silmarils was Fëanor, the eldest son of the high king of the Noldor, Finwë, and Queen Míriel. Called Curufinwë at birth, he was later named Fëanor, meaning "Spirit of Fire". He was considered the greatest of all the Eldar in gifts of mind, body and spirit. To some degree, Fëanor is comparable to the supernatural smith Ilmarinen in the Finnish epic the *Kalevala*. Ilmarinen forged the mysterious artefact known as the Sampo that brought great wealth and good fortune to its possessor. The Sampo and the Silmarils were in many respects akin to the ancient Greek cornucopia (the horn of plenty), the medieval Christian Holy

Grail, Odin's ring Draupnir and numerous other mysterious and powerful artefacts in world mythology.

Fëanor's Silmarils were three Elven gemstones filled with the sacred living light of the Trees of the Valar. These were the most beautiful and holiest gems in the world, but they were so coveted that they were first hidden away, then stolen by Melkor/Morgoth and finally became the objects of a quest to retrieve them. In that doomed pursuit of the gems into Beleriand, Fëanor was slain

Fëanor, creator of the Silmarils

and, after six centuries of warfare, the gemstones were lost: one deep under the sea, another in the bowels of the Earth, one in the upper air above the world.

The fate of the Sampo was similar to that of the Silmarils. Once created, the Sampo was first locked away in an underground vault, then stolen by a sorceress and finally became the object of a quest and battle to retrieve it, only to end up smashed and lost in the depths of the sea.

As in the Quest of the Holy Grail, Fëanor's quest to recover the Silmarils at the end of the Ages of the Stars – and its continued pursuit by his sons through the First Age of Sun in Beleriand – leads to the utter destruction of most of those who take part. Like the Grail, the Silmarils possessed a purity too great for those ensnared by the ambitions and rivalries of the world.

The Swan Haven of Alqualondë

KINGS OF ELDAMAR

PEOPLE	RULER	DWELLING PLACES
First Kindred: the Vanyar or "Fair Elves"	High King Ingwë	*Tirion and Taniquetil*
Second Kindred: the Noldor or "Deep Elves"	King Finwë (followed by Fëanor and Finarfin)	*Tirion and Formenos*
Third Kindred: the Teleri or "Sea Elves"	King Olwë	*Avallónë and Alqualondë*

KINGS OF BELERIAND IN THE AGES OF THE STARS

PEOPLE	RULER	DWELLING PLACES
Falathrim or "Elves of the Coast"	Círdan the Shipwright	*Brithombar and Eglarest*
Sindar or "Grey Elves"	High King Thingol "Greymantle"	*Menegroth, the "Thousand Caves" in the forest of Doriath*
Laiquendi or "Green Elves"	King Denethor	*Ossiriand, "Land of Seven Rivers"*

PART

THREE

HEROES OF THE FIRST AGE: ELVES AND EDAIN

THE NOLDOR
HEROES OF BELERIAND

I n Tolkien's world, when the Sun first rose in the heavens, there was an awakening of the Second Children of Eru Ilúvatar – the mortal race of Men – in the east of Middle-earth; while, in the west of Middle-earth, that same first dawn illuminated the glittering spears of the Noldor Elves of King Fingolfin as they marched into the land of Beleriand. These two races, as Tolkien relates in *The Silmarillion*, were conjoined in a common struggle that would forever determine their destinies upon Middle-earth.

The six centuries that followed the first dawn were a heroic time for the Elves and Men of Middle-earth, most comparable to the earliest ages of the Greek, Celt and Norse myths: a time when gods and other immortals – in congress with mortal men and women – undertook great adventures, battles and quests. Mortal and immortal heroes and heroines were set impossible tasks that required superhuman strength and endurance and which often ended in courageous acts of self-sacrifice.

Tolkien's history of the Noldor in Beleriand closely resembles the Irish myths of the Tuatha Dé Danann, a race of immortals who, like the Elves, did not age or suffer from sickness or disease. The Tuatha Dé Danann were the "People of the Goddess Danu", while Tolkien's Elves might be described as "People of the

Goddess Varda", the Queen of the Stars.

In their earliest days, the Tuatha Dé Danann lived in a land of immortals much as did Tolkien's Noldor Elves in Eldamar. This was Tír na nÓg, "Land of the Ever Young", whose high king, Nuada, sailed with his people over the Western Sea to the mortal shores of Ireland. There, High King Nuada burned his fleet of ships, so none of the Tuatha Dé Danann might return to Tír na nÓg.

The Silmarillion tells us of the Noldor high king Fëanor who sailed with his people over the Western Sea to the mortal shores of Beleriand. There, King Fëanor, too, burned the ships of his

The Awakening of Men at the first rising of the Sun

fleet, so none of the Noldor might return to Eldamar.

Both Nuada and Fëanor soon led their people to victory in their first battle in this new land. In advance of the rising of the first sun, the Noldor won a great victory in the Dagor-nuin-Giliath, or "Battle under Stars", but in that battle Fëanor was slain. Similarly, Nuada of the Tuatha Dé Danann led his people to victory in the First Battle of Magh Tuireadh, and – although not slain – had his arm severed, and could no longer rule as king.

So both peoples won their first battles in their new lands, but lost their king. The next high king of the Tuatha Dé Danann was the Dagda, who led his people to victory in the Second Battle of Magh Tuireadh against the monstrous legions of underworld demons and giants known as the Fomorians. In Beleriand, the next high king of the Noldor was Fingolfin, who led his people to a second victory in the Dagor Aglareb, or "Glorious Battle", against the Orcs, Trolls and Balrogs, likewise demons of the underworld.

NOLDOR KINGS AND KINGDOMS

The Dagda's victory over the Fomorian legions gave the Tuatha Dé Danann an age of relative peace during which the king's sons and those of his chieftains established fiefdoms over much of Ireland. In like manner, Fingolfin's victory over Morgoth's legions gave the Noldor nearly four centuries of relative peace. During that time Fingolfin's sons and those of his brothers, Fëanor and Finarfin, established a dozen Noldor fiefdoms in northern Beleriand as a bulwark against their foes.

However, just as the appearance of the sun signalled the beginning of the Age of Men (our historic human ancestors, Tolkien implies), it also signalled the beginning of the end of days for the Noldor upon Middle-earth. This corresponds to the history of the Tuatha Dé Danann: as their time in the mythic age of Ireland neared its end, they were eventually superseded by the Milesians, a race of mortals believed to be the ancestors of the historic Gaelic people of Ireland.

Tolkien's theme of the dwindling power of the Elves upon Middle-earth has much in common with the fading of the Tuatha Dé Danann. The remnant of this once-mighty pre-human race eventually became known as the Aes Sidhe, or the Sidhe (pronounced "Shee"). The name means the "people of the hills", for it was believed that, as these people withdrew from the mortal realm, they hid themselves away inside "hollow hills" and ancient burial mounds.

In Tolkien's Noldor and Sindar Elves of Beleriand, we have kingdoms and cities that are comparable to many of those in the legends of the Sidhe hidden away in all manner of places: in glittering caverns like King Thingol's hallowed Menegroth;

in secret valleys like Turgon's vale of Tumladen with its citadel, Gondolin; in precarious river gorges like Finrod's mighty Nargothrond; in havens like Círdan's Brithombar and Eglarest, and in distant islands like the refuge of the Isle of Balar.

NOLDOR KINGS AND KINGDOMS OF BELERIAND IN THE FIRST AGE

HOUSE	RULER	REALM
FINARFIN	Finrod Felagund	Nargothrond
	Orodreth	Tol Sirion
	Angrod and Aegnor	Dorthonion
FINGOLFIN*	Fingon	Dor-lómin
	Turgon	Nevrast and Gondolin
FËANOR	Maedhros and Maglor	Lothlann
	Celegorm and Curufin	Himlad
	Caranthir	Thargelion
	Amrod and Amras	East Beleriand

FINGOLFIN*
HIMSELF RULED
HITHLUM AND
MITHRIM

EDAIN HEROES OF BELERIAND

‒·‒·‒➤　　◄‒‒·‒·‒

T olkien's tale of the origin of Men in the east of Middle-earth and their westward migration in the Years of the Sun was a mirroring of the origin and migration of the Elves in the Years of the Trees. And, just as Tolkien's journey of the Elves was inspired by the tales related to the historic westward migrations of Celtic peoples, it can also be observed that his journey of Men was inspired by the historic westward migrations of the Teutonic peoples.

Consequently, just as the immortal Elves were aligned with the myths and folk traditions of the Celts, Tolkien's mortal Men were equally aligned with the myths and folk traditions of the Germans, Norsemen and Anglo-Saxons. The dominant language of the Elves of Beleriand was Sindarin, modelled on Welsh, while the dominant Mannish language of the Edain – those heroic Men of the First Age who entered Beleriand first – was Taliska, the ancestor of Tolkien's Third Age "common tongue" of Westron, modelled on Anglo-Saxon (Old English).

When the Edain entered Beleriand early in the fourth century of the First Age, Tolkien portrays them as a wild and proud tribal people who endured terrible trials in their westward migration. The Elves pitied these poor mortals whose span of life was brief and filled with suffering caused by age and disease. And yet,

Tolkien's Edain possess a primitive nobility and innate sense of honour that brings them close in spirit to the mortal heroes of Germanic and Norse mythology.

In the Quenya language of the Noldor, these were the Atanatári, or the "Fathers of Men", for the Edain were quick to learn the skills and crafts of the Elves and repaid their mentors with absolute loyalty and supreme acts of self-sacrifice. In these qualities, the Edain are comparable to the heroes of the Norse sagas, who were willing vassals to powerful chieftains and kings in dynastic clans or houses named after their lords. The heroes of these tales were most often the vassals rather than the ruling kings. In the case of the *Völsunga* saga, the king was Völsung, but the true heroes were his loyal vassals Sigmund and Sigurd, whose counterparts in Tolkien's Middle-earth are to be found among the Edain heroes of the House of Hador.

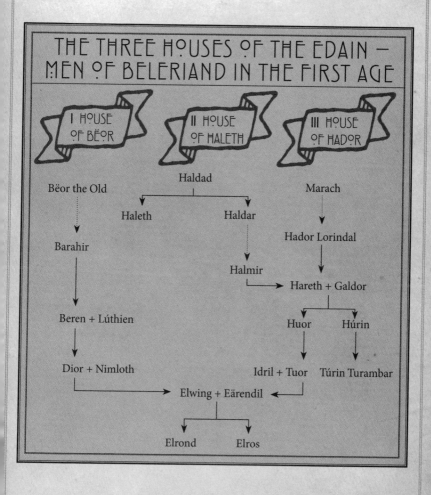

THE THREE HOUSES OF THE EDAIN — MEN OF BELERIAND IN THE FIRST AGE

I HOUSE OF BËOR

II HOUSE OF HALETH

III HOUSE OF HADOR

Bëor the Old

Haldad

Marach

Haleth   Haldar

Hador Lorindal

Barahir

Halmir

Hareth + Galdor

Beren + Lúthien

Huor   Húrin

Dior + Nimloth

Idril + Tuor   Túrin Turambar

Elwing + Eärendil

Elrond   Elros

TÚRIN THE DRAGON-SLAYER

A mong the greatest of Edain heroes of the First Age was the dragon-slayer Túrin Turambar. In good part, Tolkien's tale of Túrin and his father, Húrin, was inspired by Sigurd the dragon-slayer and his father, Sigmund, the heroes of the Völsunga saga, the Norse epic described by the nineteenth-century designer and poet William Morris as "the great story of the North, which should be to all our race what the tale of Troy was to the Greeks".

Tolkien's tale and the Norse saga begin with the deeds of the fathers. Both Húrin and Sigmund survive the near-extermination of their dynastic houses. In the Dagor Nírnaeth Arnoediad (Battle of Unnumbered Tears), Húrin is the last man standing in the Edain rearguard and, by single-handedly slaying seventy trolls, saves the retreating Noldor army from certain annihilation. With equal courage, Sigmund slaughters scores of his foes in acts of bloody revenge for the murder of his entire clan, including his eight brothers. However, both are eventually defeated: Húrin when his war axe withers in the heat of battle and Sigmund when his dynastic sword breaks in one last fatal duel.

Among the Elves and Men of Beleriand, Húrin the Steadfast was celebrated as "the mightiest warrior of mortal men" but,

Opposite: Túrin faces Glaurung on the bridge at Nargothrond

like the Norse hero Sigmund, he became even more renowned as the father of a dragon-slayer. Húrin's famous son was Túrin Turambar, the slayer of Glaurung, the Father of Dragons, while Sigmund's son was Sigurd the slayer of Fafnir, the Prince of All Dragons.

Both dragon-slayers lay claim to broken dynastic swords that were reforged: Túrin's sword was given the name Gurthang, meaning "iron of death", while Sigurd's was Gram, meaning "wrath". But, even so armed, neither of these heroes believed that these great worms could be slain by strength of arms alone. Courage and cunning were also required to defeat this terror. Túrin chose to hide himself in a deep ravine at a river crossing, and, when Glaurung attempted to cross over the gap, he drove his sword upward and into the massive monster's underbelly. Sigurd hid himself in a covered trench dug into the narrow road the beast took each day to drink from a forest pool: when Fafnir's great body passed over the trench, the Völsung hero drove his sword Gram up into the dragon's exposed belly.

The Dwarf-mines of Belegost

DWARVES OF BELERIAND

I n *The Hobbit*, the reader's initial impression of Thorin and
his company is largely consistent with the dwarfs of the
mildly comic fairy-tale variety. However, the Dwarves in *The
Silmarillion* are a rather dark and brooding race with the fatalistic
character of the Dwarf-smiths of Norse mythology.

Although Tolkien gives a brief account of the awakening of
the Seven Fathers of the Dwarves in the Years of the Trees and
provides some mention of their traffic and trade, no account
of a true hero of that secretive race emerges until the Dagor
Nírnaeth Arnoediad in the War of the Jewels. In that battle,
Tolkien reveals his Dwarves as master forgers of arms and
armour, just like the Dwarf-smiths in Norse mythology. Armed
with their mighty war axes, the Dwarves of Belegost, masked in
dwarf-helms and clothed in flame-proof coats of Dwarf-mail,
stubbornly hold their ground against the all-consuming fire of

the dragon Glaurung and his brood. Tolkien also reveals that during this battle, in addition to demonstrating their skills as smiths, the Dwarves also showed themselves to be a fierce race of warriors, which marks them apart from the fairy-tale stereotype. For example, though it cost him his life, in his dying moments the Dwarf king Azaghâl drove his dagger deep into the belly of Glaurung and forced him and his brood from the field.

Tolkien's portrayal of his Dwarves was inspired by a desire to distinguish this race from the latter-day use of the term "dwarf" to describe human beings of diminutive stature, and connect them instead with the bearded, short, stocky beings of Germanic mythology who lived in caverns beneath mountains. Tolkien began his attempt to define his race by recognizing a proper plural term for these people and came up with "Dwarves", all the while acknowledging that, from a linguistic perspective, it would be more correct to call them "Dwarrows". By exploring traditional fairy tales, Tolkien also attempted to discover more about this race: the connection of dwarfs with mines, the hoarding of treasure, the forging of supernatural weapons, and the creation of jewellery and gifts with magical attributes. All of these aspects, to a greater or lesser degree, contributed to Tolkien's reinvention of Dwarves for Middle-earth.

THE QUEST OF THE SILMARIL

As Tolkien saw it, "there is a strand of 'blood' and inheritance, derived from the Elves, and the art and poetry of Men is largely dependent on it, or modified by it". In his stories, the wisdom and history of the immortal Elves constitute the inheritance of Men from the age of myth – an inheritance that provides the ennobling spirit of human civilization. Crucial to establishing that link between Elves and Men was the betrothal of the Elven princess Lúthien to the mortal hero Beren, a betrothal that forced them into the Quest of the Silmaril.

Lúthien was the daughter of Elu Thingol, the high king of the Grey Elves and his queen, Melian the Maia. She was considered the most beautiful child of any race and the fairest singer within the spheres of the world, about whom nightingales gathered. For this, she was named Lúthien Tinúviel, meaning "maiden of twilight", and was the very embodiment of the enchanting "lady in white" so often portrayed in Celtic legend.

In the Welsh legend of the wooing of Olwyn, we have another maiden who is considered the most beautiful woman of her age. Her eyes, like Lúthien's, shine with light; her skin is also as white as snow. Olwyn's name means "she of the white track" – a name she earned because four white trefoils sprang up on the forest floor with every step she took. Compare the legend of this flower to Tolkien's Niphredil, a white star-shaped flower that first bloomed on Middle-earth in celebration of Lúthien's birth, and later blossomed eternally on her burial mound. The winning of Olwyn's hand required her suitor, Culhwch, to undertake the near-impossible quest of the "Thirteen Treasures of Britain", and this is certainly comparable to the near-impossible Quest of the Silmaril, the price for Lúthien's hand being one of the three Silmarils in the crown of Morgoth, the Dark Enemy.

However, an even more obvious source of inspiration for Tolkien's Quest of the Silmaril was the ancient Greek love story of Orpheus and Eurydice. Both Tolkien's tale and the Greek myth concern themselves with a descent into the underworld and the power of love and music in the face of death. In Tolkien's version, Lúthien sang and made Carcharoth the wolf-guardian fall asleep before the gates of Morgoth's dark subterranean fortress. Once within, Lúthien once again sang such beautiful songs that the entranced Morgoth fell into a slumber, thus enabling Beren to cut one of the Silmaril jewels from his iron crown. Lúthien succeeded in fleeing from Angband, but at the last moment, at the mouth of the tunnel, she lost her lover Beren.

In Tolkien's adaptation of the Greek myth, the male and female roles are reversed. In the Greek myth, Orpheus played his harp and sang to make Cerberus the hound-guardian fall asleep before the gates of Hades. Once within, Orpheus again sang such beautiful songs that Hades wept and granted him the life of

Beren cuts the Silmaril from Morgoth's crown

Eurydice. Orpheus succeeded in fleeing from the underworld, but at the last moment, at the mouth of the tunnel, his lover Eurydice is taken from him and returned to Hades.

To underscore the connection between the Greek myth and

his tale, Tolkien duplicates the journey by having Lúthien pursue
Beren's soul after his death. This time, in the real House of the
Dead in the Undying Lands, Lúthien exactly repeats Orpheus's
journey by singing to Mandos-Hades and winning a second life
for her lover. Unlike Orpheus and Eurydice, however, Lúthien
and Beren are allowed to live out their newly won mortal lives.
And so, in the Quest of the Silmaril, Tolkien not only reversed
the roles of Orpheus and Eurydice, but also overturned that
story's tragic end. And in so doing, for a time at least, Tolkien
allowed love to conquer death.

THE VOYAGE OF EÄRENDIL

I t all began with a star. In antiquity, it was the "morning star".
It was also the "evening star"; that is, the planet we now
know as Venus – named after the Roman goddess of love. In
1913, while still a student of Oxford, the young J. R. R. Tolkien
discovered this bright star in the text of an Old English (Anglo-
Saxon) mystical poem known as the *Christ of Cynewulf*: "Hail
Eärendel brightest of angels / Above the middle-earth sent unto
men." From this context, Tolkien deduced that Eärendel must
refer to the morning star itself, shining above the land of men
midway between heaven and hell, otherwise known as "Middle-
earth".

Opposite: Lúthien finds Beren

In Eärendil, "brightest of angels", Tolkien believed that he
had discovered an original Old English myth. This was the myth
behind an obscure fragment of a surviving Icelandic fairy tale,
a story about the heroic Orentil, who in Norse mythology was
identified with the morning star. Over the next year, Tolkien
set himself the task of imaginatively reconstructing what he
considered the true myth of Eärendil. The end result was
Tolkien's composition of a long narrative poem, entitled "The
Voyage of Eärendil".

Tolkien's Eärendil – like an ancient Flying Dutchman – is
a mariner who wanders through an endless maze of shadowy
seas and enchanted isles. As the emissary of the Elves and Edain
of Beleriand, Eärendil sailed in search of the Undying Lands.
Tolkien's tale is also like that of the Flying Dutchman in that his
mariner's ultimate salvation and deliverance are achieved only
through a self-sacrificing act on the part of his maiden lover. In
Tolkien's tale, the mariner's lover was the Elven princess Elwing
of Doriath, the granddaughter of Beren and Lúthien Tinúviel,
and the inheritor of the Silmaril.

Leaping to seemingly certain death from a high cliff into the
sea, Elwing is magically transformed into a seabird that flies
to Eärendil, carrying the holy jewel of living light in her beak.
And so, with the Silmaril bound to his brow and lighting the
way, Eärendil succeeds at last in steering his ship through to the
shores of the Undying Lands.

Tolkien wrote "The Voyage of Eärendil" in the late summer of 1914 as his first venture into what would eventually become his invented world of Arda. In that poem, and later in *The Silmarillion*, Eärendil is lifted into the firmament where the radiant light of the Silmaril – as the morning star – shines down forever after on Tolkien's Middle-earth. For, although his poem had its genesis in the lines of another poem from another time, as Humphrey Carpenter explained in his biography of the author, Tolkien had created in Eärendil something uniquely his own – and more besides. As Carpenter put it, "It was in fact the beginning of Tolkien's own mythology."

THE WAR OF WRATH

The mission of Eärendil the Mariner, in which he crossed the Western Sea on behalf of the Free Peoples of Middle-earth, resulted in an alliance with the Valarian Powers of Arda to fight Morgoth, the Dark Enemy. For the first time, all the heroes of Middle-earth and the Undying Lands were drawn together as a single force in a final conflict that owes, as Tolkien once stated, "more to the Norse vision of Ragnarök than anything else".

This conflict was known as the War of Wrath in which Manwë, the king of the Valar, sent Valar, Maiar, Vanyar and Noldor warriors of Aman into battle in Middle-earth against

Morgoth and his allies. This war was comparable to the Norse Ragnarök, a future final struggle in which Odin, the king of the gods, will send Æsir, Vanir, valkyries and einherjar (the fallen warriors of Valhalla) of Asgard into battle in Midgard against Loki, the Norse god of chaos. Tolkien's Morgoth is certainly comparable to the vengeful Loki, the harbinger of Ragnarök. Both are held captive for long ages in chains and, upon being freed, unleash dark and monstrous forces on the world.

The surviving Sindar, Noldor, Edain and Dwarves of Beleriand fought alongside the mighty Valarian host for four decades in a conflict that culminated in one last battle before the gates of Angband. Tolkien's cataclysmic Great Battle began when Eönwë, the Herald of the Valar, sounded his battle horn, while the slaughter of Ragnarök will begin when Heimdall the watchmen of the Æsir sounds his battle horn. Similarly, in *The Silmarillion* we have Morgoth's champion, the terrible Gothmog, with his sword of flame, leading his legions of Balrogs, "demons of fire", while in the Völuspá – the Norse poem which describes the creation of the world – we have Loki's champion, the titanic Surt with his sword of flame leading his legions of *eldjötnar* ("fire giants"). In Ragnarök, we have the horrific Fenrir, the greatest wolf of Midgard, who swallowed the Sun, while in Tolkien we have the monstrous Carcharoth, the greatest wolf of Middle-earth, who swallowed the Silmaril. In Ragnarök, the Midgard Serpent, Jörmungand, sprays venom over the sea, while in the

Opposite: Glaurung at the Fifth Battle

Great Battle the dragons breathe fire over the land.

Some aspects of these tales are antithetical in nature: in Tolkien, we have the Hammer of the Underworld, Grond, in the hands of Morgoth, the Vala of earthquakes and darkness, while in the Norse legends we have the Hammer of the Gods, Mjölnir – meaning "Grinder" – in the hands of Thor, the god of thunder and lightning. In Middle-earth we have Huan, the valiant Hound of the Valar, while in Midgard we have Garm, the evil Hound of the goddess Hel.

However, as the tide of that last Great Battle turned slowly but relentlessly against the forces of the Dark Lord, Morgoth unleashed his ultimate weapon – Ancalagon the Black, the largest and most powerful dragon in the history of Arda – and, in his wake, a legion of winged dragons flew out from the pits of Angband and drove the Valarian host back.

The attack of Ancalagon (meaning "rushing jaws") in the Great Battle has a precedent, in Völuspá's account of Ragnarök, in "the flying dragon, glowing serpent" known as Nithhogg (meaning "malice striker"), a monster that will emerge from the dark underworld of Niflheim, where it has long gnawed at the roots of the world tree.

The aerial attack of Nithhogg, combined with the sea assault led by Loki at the helm of Naglfar, the great "Ship of the Dead" made from the fingernails and toenails of human corpses and captained by the *jötunn* (giant) Hrym, will turn the tide of battle against the gods. This dual threat will result in the mutually assured destruction of both Odin's gods and Loki's giants – and, ultimately, the entire Norse cosmos.

In Tolkien's Great Battle, however, the aerial attack of Ancalagon and his legion of winged dragons was met by an aerial counterattack by Eärendil the Mariner at the helm of his great flying ship, hallowed by the Valar and lifted into the heavens. In the end, Eärendil slew Ancalagon, and the host of the Valar was victorious.

And so, although the War of Wrath ended in victory for the Valarian host, the price of that victory was the total destruction of all the kingdoms and lands of Beleriand. To some degree, both Tolkien and the Norsemen shared a cataclysmic vision of the fate of their worlds, but neither vision was ultimately without hope. In both, we learn something of how the sunken and drowned world is raised again from the ocean floor, and a green and fruitful land appears. In the Norse cosmos, this was the shining vision of Gimlé with its roof of gold, while in Tolkien's world this was the island continent of Númenor.

Next page: Ancalagon the Black Dragon is slain by Earendil

PART

FOUR

HEROES OF THE
SECOND AGE:
NOLDOR AND
NÚMENÓREANS

THE SEA KINGS OF NÚMENOR

The Second Age is the age of the mighty Sea Kings of Númenor. These are the rulers of the surviving Edain of Beleriand who are given refuge on the island-continent of Andor ("Land of the Gift") in Belegaer, the Sundering Sea, between Middle-earth and the Undying Lands. The island is also known as Elenna-nórë, or "Land of the Star", as it is roughly shaped like a pentagram. As Tolkien undoubtedly knew, this five-pointed star was the sacred symbol of the ancient Greek mystical sect known as the Pythagoreans. This was known as the "Star of Man" because its five points relate to an outstretched body: the head at the top, the arms and hands at the side, and the legs and feet at the bottom.

The first Númenórean king, Elros, and his brother, Elrond, are the twin sons of a mortal man, Eärendil the Mariner, and an immortal Elven maid, Elwing the White. Known as the Peredhil ("Half-elven") because of their mixed blood, they are allowed to choose their race and fate: the mortal world of Men or the immortal world of Elves. Elrond chooses to be immortal and eventually becomes the elven lord of Imladris in Middle-earth. His brother Elros chooses to be mortal (though allowed a lifespan of five centuries) and becomes the founding king of the Númenóreans.

Elros and Elrond have their counterparts in the Greek myth of the twin brothers Castor and Pollux. Known as the Dioscuri ("divine twins"), these heroes were the sons of the mortal woman Leda and the immortal god Zeus. In this case, Castor was a mortal man and Pollux an immortal god. When the mortal brother Castor was slain in battle, his immortal brother Pollux was filled with grief because he could never be reunited with his brother, even in the Underworld. Zeus took pity on them and transformed the brothers into the constellation Gemini, the Heavenly Twins.

Tolkien's twins are not reunited and placed among the stars. However, there is a star connection in the figure of Elros and Elrond's father, Eärendil the Mariner. As we have observed in Part 3, Eärendil was originally an obscure figure in Teutonic

The Númenórean port of Andúnië

myth whom Jacob Grimm associated with the morning star; in Tolkien's tales, Eärendil the Mariner binds the shining Silmaril to his brow and forever rides his flying ship through the firmament, where, in the form of the morning star, he guides all sailors and travellers.

Tolkien's Akallabêth, which relates the downfall and destruction of Númenor, is his reinvention of the ancient Greek Atlantis legend. This was one very distinct case of Tolkien taking an ancient legend and rewriting it in such a way as to suggest that this is the real history on which a myth was based. So that we do not miss the point, Tolkien tells us that the High Elven (Quenya) form of Númenor is Atalantë, meaning "the downfallen".

Tolkien often mentioned that he had "an Atlantis complex", which took the form of a "terrible recurrent dream of the Great Wave, towering up, and coming in ineluctably over the trees and green fields". He appeared to believe that this was some kind of race memory of the ancient catastrophe of the sinking of Atlantis. He stated on more than one occasion that he had inherited this dream from his parents, and that it had been passed on to his son, Michael. Through writing the Akallabêth, however, Tolkien found that he had finally managed to exorcise this disturbing dream.

The original legend of Atlantis comes from Plato's dialogue *Timaeus* (c 360 BCE) in which an Egyptian priest talks to the Athenian statesman Solon. The priest tells Solon that the mightiest civilization the world had ever known existed nine thousand years before his time in the island-kingdom of Atlantis. Atlantis was an island about the size of Spain in the Western Sea beyond the Pillars of Heracles. Its power extended over all the nations of Europe and the Mediterranean, but the overwhelming pride of these powerful people brought them into conflict with the immortals. Finally, a great cataclysm in the form of a volcanic

Elros Tar-Minyatúr, the first king of Númenor

eruption and a tidal wave resulted in Atlantis sinking beneath the sea.

Tolkien used Plato's legend as an outline for the Akallabêth. However, Tolkien seemed incapable of doing what most authors would have done – simply writing a straight dramatic narrative based on the legend. Instead, he added little personal touches and background details for his lost island: that is to say, the compilation of three thousand years of detailed history, sociology, geography, natural history, linguistics and biography.

SEA KINGS OF NÚMENOR

Eärendil the Mariner

Elros Tar-Minyatur
First King of Númenor
S.A. 32–442

Tar-Elendil
Fourth King of Númenor
Elf-friend of Gil-galad
S.A. 590–740

Valandil
First Lord of Andúnië
S.A. 630–870

*The War of the
Elves and Sauron*
1695–1701

Tar-Minastir
Eleventh King
Established the Havens of Umbar
S.A. 1731–1869

Ar-Pharazôn
Twenty-fifth King
"The Usurper"
S.A. 3255–3319

Amandil
Eighteenth Lord of Andúnië
SAILED WEST S.A. 3316

Elendil the Tall
Nineteenth Lord of Andúnië
SAILED EAST S.A. 3319

S.A. 3319 THE DOWNFALL OF NÚMENOR

Númenórean realms in exile
Elendil in Arnor
Isildur and Anárion in Gondor
FROM S.A. 3320

TOLKIEN'S DREAM AND HISTORY

Tolkien's creation of Númenor – or "Westernesse" in the common tongue of Westron – was his conscious attempt to reinvent the "true history" behind the destruction of Atlantis, a legend that is shared by many of the world's mythologies. Tolkien was almost too clever in the way he wove his tale. However much Tolkien worked the story into a "legend on the brink of fairy tale and history", at the same time he obviously believed in the destruction of Atlantis as a genuine historic event.

Remarkably, Tolkien managed to live just long enough to have the historicity of the sudden cataclysmic destruction of an Atlantis-like civilization proved accurate, as well as his description of the "Great Wave" that followed in its wake. In the mid-1960s excavations in the Aegean revealed an island kingdom that had been destroyed in the second millennium BCE by a volcanic eruption and a great wave. This tidal wave devastated the entire Mediterranean from Greece to Morocco and Spain and was undoubtedly the historic event that inspired Plato's tale of Atlantis. Thera – today known as Santorini – had been a centre of Minoan culture, yet it – together with many of the Minoan settlements on nearby Crete – was all but destroyed by a cataclysmic event in the course of a single day. The age of the

Opposite: Sunrise on Númenor

Minoan sea kings came to an end as the largest tidal wave ever witnessed by humankind swept through the Mediterranean.

So it seems that this terror of the Great Wave had flooded out of Tolkien's personal nightmare into a legend, then into Middle-earth, before bursting back in upon human history. Or perhaps, as Tolkien suggested, the sequence ran in the opposite order, beginning in Middle-earth. Whatever the case, Tolkien's belief in this recurring dream did result in the composition of the annals of the Sea Kings of Númenor and their kingdom, which in later days, in Tolkien's mythology, was known by the ancient Greeks as Atlantis.

However, that was not the nightmare's end. Just as Tolkien's own son, Michael, inherited the dream, so we discover in *The Lord of the Rings* that, millennia later, a descendant of the Sea Kings has inherited a horrific vision of the downfall of Númenor. During the War of the Ring, Faramir watches the destruction of Sauron, and confesses that it reminds him of his recurring dream "of the great dark wave climbing over green lands ... coming on, darkness inescapable".

NÚMENÓREAN REALMS IN EXILE: ARNOR AND GONDOR

J ust as the story of the disaster of Atlantis has echoes in many mythologies from around the world, there are an equal number of legends concerning the survivors of such cataclysms and the creation of new kingdoms in new lands. The Aztec of Mexico, for example, claimed to be descendants of those who escaped the submerging of an Atlantis-like continent named Aztlán. Celtic tales tell of ancestors originating from the sunken land of Cantref Gwaelod in present-day Cardigan Bay, off the west coast of Wales. In ancient Greece, the tale of Deucalion and Pyrrha's survival of the Great Flood is almost identical to that of Noah and his wife in the Bible, the couples' offspring repopulating the world.

In Tolkien's world, Elendil the Tall, as leader of the Faithful, and the last Lord of Andúnië, survives the downfall of Númenor. And just as Virgil in the *Aeneid* wrote of how Aeneas, the last Trojan prince, survived the downfall of Troy and sailed west to Italy where his descendants founded the great city and empire of Rome, so Tolkien's histories tell of how Elendil, the last Númenórean prince, sails east to Middle-earth where he and his sons, Isildur and Anarian, found the mighty Númenórean Realms in Exile – the North-kingdom of Arnor and the South-kingdom of Gondor.

The Pillars of the Kings

LAST KINGDOM OF THE NOLDOR ELVES

J ust as the Edain of Beleriand become the founders of the kingdom of Númenor, so the Elves who survive the War of Wrath gather in the last Noldor kingdom in Middle-earth to the west of the Blue Mountains – the kingdom of Lindon and the Grey Havens. There they rally under the banner of Gil-galad – meaning "radiant star" – the last high king of the Noldor who, Tolkien informs us, carries the Elf-forged spear Aeglos, meaning "snow point" or "icicle", that "none may stand before". Aeglos was undoubtedly meant by Tolkien to be an allusion to the mythical spear Gungnir, the symbol of the power and authority of Odin, the Norse king of the gods. Gungnir, forged in Alfheim by the elf-smith Dwalin, was considered the most fearful weapon of the Lord of Victories.

Gil-galad is the high king of Lindon, but it is Círdan the Shipwright who is the harbourmaster of the Grey Havens and builder of the swan ships of the Elves, which alone – after the Change of the World – are capable of sailing the "Straight Road" to Avallónë in the Undying Lands. Avallónë (meaning "near Valinor") on the Lonely Isle of Tol Eressëa was certainly (as Tolkien acknowledged in a letter to his publisher) an allusion to King Arthur's immortal realm of Avalon.

Tolkien was also quite clear about the origin and the telltale geography of Lindon and the Grey Havens. As he indicated, the Welsh mountains on the border of the English Midlands are comparable to the Blue Mountains on the border of Eriador. We need only glance at the geography of the coastlines of Wales and Cornwall severed by that distinctive wedge of the Bristol Channel and the River Severn to see the geography duplicated in the coastlines of North and South Lindon, severed by a similarly distinctive wedge created by the Gulf of Lune and the river Lhûn (Lune).

As a child in the rural Midlands, Tolkien became interested in the strange language written on the sides of Welsh coal trucks. He developed an aesthetic sense in language, believing that some languages were "beautiful" and others "ugly". Upon hearing Welsh spoken and sung in church choirs, Tolkien had no doubt that in Welsh he had discovered one of the world's most beautiful and musical of languages. If Elves had a language, Tolkien believed it was logical to look for its origins in the language of these original Britons. Consequently, as we have already observed, he invented an Elven language (Sindar) that was based on the structure of Welsh.

The history, myths and languages of ancient Wales and Elvish Lindon became two sides of the same coin to Tolkien. The choirs of Wales are renowned throughout the world, while Lindon is the "land of song". Historically, Wales and Cornwall were the last refuges of the true "British" – as distinct from the "English" – people, just as North and South Lindon are the last true refuges of the High Elves of Middle-earth.

This distinction between British and English is critical to understanding Middle-earth's cosmology. Tolkien insisted that, properly speaking, the term "British" refers to the Welsh-speaking Celts who settled the land at least two millennia before the arrival of the relatively primitive English (Anglo-Saxon) tribes in the fifth century CE. Through many centuries of contact and government under the Romans, most aristocratic Britons and all the British clergy spoke Latin. Tolkien was well aware of this, and wrote of how the Sindar language was created to resemble Welsh, while the Quenya language of the Noldor Elves was invented to resemble a kind of Elvish Latin. Curiously, Tolkien chose Finnish – a difficult language with complex inflections – as the basis for the native tongue of Gil-galad and the Noldor Elves of Lindon and the Noldor and Vanyar of Eldamar in the Undying Lands.

ELVEN KINGDOMS OF MIDDLE-EARTH IN THE SECOND AGE

FOUNDED IN	KINGDOM	FOUNDED BY
S.A. 1	Lindon/Forlindon	GIL-GALAD d. S.A. 1697, during the War of the Elves and Sauron
	Mithlond/Grey Havens	CÍRDAN THE SHIPWRIGHT
	Harlindon	GALADRIEL AND CELEBORN
S.A. 750 ONWARDS	Eryn Galen/Greenwood	OROPHER d. S.A. 3434, during the Battle of Dagorlad
	Lórien/Lórinand	AMDIR d. S.A. 3434, during the Battle of Dagorlad
S.A. 750–1350	Eregion/Hollin	GALADRIEL AND CELEBORN
S.A. 1350–1697	Eregion/Hollin	CELEBRIMBOR d. S.A. 1697, during the War of the Elves and Sauron
S.A. 1697 ONWARDS	Imladris/Rivendell	ELROND HALF-ELVEN

CELEBRIMBOR AND THE RINGS OF POWER

The belief in the supernatural power of rings has been with humanity since the dawn of history. Tales of such rings are to be found in myths and folk literature of nations throughout the world. Furthermore, this belief in supernatural rings did not restrict itself to legends and fairy tales; it is very much a part of history itself.

Likewise, in Tolkien's Middle-earth the history and fate of Elves and Men in the Second and Third Ages are in large part determined by the struggle over the possession of the Rings of Power forged by the Gwaith-i-Mírdain, "the Elven Smiths" of Eregion, and, above all, of the One Ring, forged by Sauron in the fires of Mount Doom. The One Ring is comparable in its powers and significance to the ring worn by Odin, the Norse king of the gods and ruler of the Nine Worlds. Odin's Draupnir is his wealth and power.

In Tolkien's tale, all the skill of Celebrimbor (meaning "Silver Fist"), lord of the Gwaith-i-Mírdain and the greatest smith of Middle-earth, and all the guile of Sauron went into the forging of the Rings of Power. In Norse myth, all the skill of Sindri and Brokkr, the greatest smiths in the Nine Worlds, and all the wisdom of Odin, were invested in the forging of Draupnir.

Draupnir means "the dripper", for this magical golden ring has the power to drip eight other rings of equal size every nine days. Its possession by Odin is not only emblematic of his dominion over the Nine Worlds but consolidates his accumulated powers by giving him a source of almost infinite wealth. This scenario seems to be fairly suggestive of Tolkien's "Nine Rings of Mortal Men", which Sauron uses to buy the allegiance of the Men of Middle-earth, and ultimately entrap their souls.

Through Draupnir, Odin rules Asgard, while the other eight rings are used as gifts of wealth and power through which the other eight worlds (including Midgard, or "Middle-earth") are governed. In Tolkien, of course, we have the addition of the Seven Rings of the Dwarves and the Three Rings of the Elves – and a dispute over their possession that leads inevitably to the terrible War of the Elves and Sauron.

Opposite: Celebrimbor forging one of the Rings of Power

CELEBRIMBOR AND
THE RINGS OF POWER

Mahtan
"Copper Lover"

Míriel
"Jewel Daughter"

Finwë, *High King of the Noldor*

Nerdanel the Wise
Sculptor

Fëanor
*"Spirit of Fire",
maker of the Silmarils*

Curufin
"Skilful Son"

Celebrimbor
*"Silver Fist",
forger of the Rings of Power*

NINE RINGS
OF MEN
(CELEBRIMBOR)

THREE RINGS
OF ELVES
(CELEBRIMBOR)

SEVEN RINGS
OF DWARVES
(CELEBRIMBOR)

The Witch-king of
Angmar

–

Khamûl the
Black Easterling

–

(Three) The Black
Númenóreans

–

(Four) The Easterlings
and Southrons

*Nenya, the white Ring of Water
– wielded by Galadriel*

–

*Vilya, the blue Ring of Air –
wielded by Elrond*

–

*Narya, the red Ring of Fire –
wielded by Círdan*

Longbeards
(Durin's Folk)

–

Broadbeams

–

Firebeards

–

Ironfists

–

Stiffbeards

–

Blacklocks

–

Stonefoots

THE ONE RING
(SAURON)

LAST ALLIANCE OF ELVES AND MEN

The first year of the Second Age is the date of High King Gil-galad's founding of Lindon, while the last year of the Second Age (S.A. 3441) is the date of his fatal duel with Sauron the Ring Lord. This was the last battle in the Last Alliance of Elves and Men, continuing a classic theme in Tolkien's writing that is redolent of other last battles in many other epic mythological traditions.

The Battle of Camlann brought an end to the Arthurian Age, and fulfilled a requirement common to epic poetry and romance, whereby the lost golden age of heroes and heroines ends in cataclysm. In the *Iliad*, Homer sang of the destruction of Troy, of the slaughter of its people and the obliteration of its civilization. In the Norse *Völsunga* saga and the German epic of the *Nibelungenlied*, similar final conflicts end tragically with the extinction of the entire Völsung and Nibelung dynasties.

In the Last Alliance of Elves and Men, Tolkien strategically places Gil-galad, high king of the Noldor, and Elendil, high king of the Númenóreans-in-Exile, on the battleground in a fatal duel with Sauron the Ring Lord and his Ringwraiths on the slopes of Mount Doom in Mordor. This is the climax to Tolkien's epic tales of the Second Age, and is most obviously comparable to the alliance of the Knights of the Round Table in the Battle of

Camlann where a similar fatal duel is fought between Arthur, high king of the Britons, and Mordred, the lord of an alliance of Picts, Scots and Saxons.

Although the dark forces of both Mordred and Sauron are destroyed, the cost to the victors is so great that what follows is centuries of chaos and warfare. In Britain, King Arthur and the greater part of the Knights of the Round Table are slain. The dream of Camelot is ended. In Middle-earth, Gil-galad and the greater part of the Alliance of Elves and Men are slain. In Britain, victory brought ruin to the dream of the kingdom of Camelot while, in Middle-earth, victory brings ruin to the kingdoms of Elves and Men.

Worse still, on Middle-earth, the One Ring is not destroyed after that last battle. For like that famously cursed Ring of Andvari in the Norse *Völsunga* saga that is claimed by Hreidmar, the king of the dwarves, "as wereguild for his son Otr's death", so the terrible One Ring of Sauron is claimed by Isildur, sole surviving son of Elendil, "as wereguild for my father's death, and my brother's". Disastrously, the evil of these rings soon results in the treacherous murders of both Hreidmar and Isildur, and their terrible curses will be passed down through generations to come.

Elendil, Isildur and Anárion of the Dúnedain

PART
FIVE

HEROES OF THE THIRD AGE: PART I. DÚNEDAIN AND DWARVES

THE KINGS OF GONDOR AND ARNOR

Tolkien's tales of the Third Age are concerned primarily with the fate of the Númenóreans-in-Exile: the United Kingdom of the Dúnedain ("Men of the West") that, with the death of High King Isildur (in T.A. 2), is divided – or, as Tolkien phrased it, "sundered" – into the two kingdoms of Gondor and Arnor.

"Sundering" is a word that recurs in Tolkien's works – most often in reference to the kingdoms of the Elves, Dwarves and Men – and is nearly always associated with tragic consequences. The theme of division was clearly something that affected him profoundly. In his stories, there are many examples of the distress, turmoil and disasters that arise from division. One of the main strands of his thought is apparent here: division leads to tragedy, or at the very least, as with the eventual retreat of the Elves from Middle-earth, to mourning and melancholy. Unification, if it can be achieved, leads to positive results, joy and contentment.

Of course, the "return of the king" – the restoration of a lost dynasty – is a recurring theme not only in mythology but in the real-world history of most nations with hereditary monarchs. Some "returns" ultimately prove successful, as in the case of Charles II (1630–85) in England, while others end in failure, as with "Bonnie" Prince Charlie (1720–88), the "King-over-the-

Water", in Scotland. But, in the end, there remains the dream – and, in Tolkien's world, it is the survival of a royal Númenórean bloodline that keeps alive the hope of the "return of the king" that promises to reunite a sundered people. Just as the historic Jacobites kept the Stuart claim to the British throne alive for over a century, Tolkien's Chieftains of Arnor in the north and Stewards of Gondor in the south keep their faith in the eventual return of a true king for over a thousand years.

Isildur with the One Ring

Tolkien certainly draws from his extensive knowledge of sundered and reunited kingdoms in myth and history for parallels to his own history of Middle-earth. The loss at sea of Arvedui, the last king of Arthedain (the last surviving realm of Arnor), with the wreck of the Elven swan ship in T.A. 1975, resonates with the historic *White Ship* disaster in 1120 that extinguished the only legitimate heirs to the English throne. The acceptance of a challenge to fight the Witch-king in mortal combat by Eärnur, the last king of Gondor, and his subsequent disappearance in the Dark Tower, may owe something of its inspiration to the Victorian poet Robert Browning's "Childe Roland to the Dark Tower Came" (1855).

Curiously enough, in one of his letters, Tolkien compares the struggle of the North- and South-kingdoms of the Dúnedain towards unity with the efforts of the Egyptian pharaohs to unite the North and South Kingdoms of Egypt. This comparison is made explicit in his design for the double crown of his Reunited Kingdom, which was based on that of an Egyptian pharaoh. In that same letter Tolkien explains: "I think the crown of Gondor (the South-Kingdom) was very tall, like that of Egypt, but with wings attached, not set straight back but at an angle. The North Kingdom had only a diadem – cf. the difference between the North and South kingdoms of Egypt. "

However, the most obvious historical precedent for the Dúnedain kingdoms of Gondor and Arnor in the Third Age can be found in the rise and fall of the Roman Empire – and its eventual resurrection in the form of the Holy Roman Empire. If one looks to the history of Rome, it is not difficult to discover similarities with this ancient imperial power in the chronicles of Middle-earth; there are certainly many aspects of Rome's history specifically comparable to the ancient history of Gondor. To begin with, the founders of both city-states are brothers. Just as the foundations of Rome were laid by twin brothers, Romulus and Remus, so too, the kingdom of Gondor was founded by two brothers (although not twins), Isildur and Anárion.

There are other similarities. Observing the division of the

Tarannon, the first Ship-king of Gondor

historic Western Roman Empire and the Eastern Byzantine Empire, it is reasonably easy to match them up with Gondor and Arnor. The disastrous military and social history of the North-kingdom, Arnor, and its subsequent collapse is comparable to the history of the Western Roman Empire. They differ mostly because the fall of the historic Empire in the West was more rapid, and far more brutal. Likewise, the North-kingdom's waning and division into the three successor states of Arthedain, Rhudaur and Cardolan is somewhat imitative of the fate of the Western Roman Empire's demise and division into its three spheres of influence – Italy, Germany and France.

However, by the end of the Third Age, after three millennia of conflict, Tolkien presents the reader with a remarkable hero – comparable to the historic Charlemagne – who is also the legitimate heir to the double crown of the kingdoms of Arnor and Gondor. In so doing, Tolkien implicitly suggests and explicitly states that, in his chronicles of Middle-earth, the progress of the histories of Arnor and Gondor was based on the historic precedent of "the re-establishment of an effective Holy Roman Empire."

Guardsman of Minas Tirith

KINGS OF GONDOR AND ARNOR

Elendil the Tall
First High King
d. S.A. 3441

↓

Isildur
Second High King
d. T.A. 2

KINGS OF ARNOR
Line of Isildur

Valandil: *Third King*
d. T.A. 249

Arvedui
Fifteenth and last King
d. T.A. 1975

**Chieftains of
the Dúnedain**

Aranarth
First Chieftain
d. T.A. 2106

Aragorn II
Sixteenth and last Chieftain
d. F.A. 120

KINGS OF GONDOR
Line of Anárion

Meneldil: *Third King*
d. T.A. 156

Eärnur
Thirty-fourth and last King
d. T.A. 2050

**Ruling Stewards
of Gondor**

Mardil the Steadfast
First Steward
d. T.A. 2080

Denethor II
Twenty-second and last Steward
d. T.A. 3019

Boromir
d. T.A. 3019

Faramir
d. F.A. 82

THE ORIGINAL TOLKIEN

T olkien saw his personal mythology linked to the Holy
Roman Empire through his mother's early Mercian-English
ancestors, and later through his father's Austrian-German
ancestors. Tolkien's claims to ancestral connections with the Holy
Roman Empire were suspiciously symmetrical. For just as he
imagined that his mother's Mercian ancestors might have fought
in Charlemagne's Imperial Army against the Moorish invasion of
Europe in the eighth century, he also imagined that his father's
ancestry was linked to the Holy Roman Empire at the time of the
Ottoman invasion of Europe in the sixteenth.

A Tolkien family legend claimed that the "original"
Tolkien had been an officer in the Imperial cavalry of the
Holy Roman Empire – comparable to the Rohan cavalry, allies
of the Dúnedain of Gondor. His name had been Georg von
Hohenzollern, and it was claimed he had fought alongside
Archduke Ferdinand of Austria against the invading Turks at
the Siege of Vienna in 1529 – a siege that was broken by an
unexpected and ferocious cavalry charge that turned the tide
of war, and ultimately brought an end to Ottoman ambitions in
Europe.

It was claimed that, during the siege, von Hohenzollern made
a series of flamboyant cavalry raids that were so outrageously

dangerous that he earned the nickname Tollkühn, meaning "foolhardy". It was a tale Tolkien deprecated all his life, but secretly it delighted him. He often retold the tale in disguised form so obscurely that virtually none of his readers or members of his lecture audiences registered his private little joke. On several occasions he used the name "Rashbold", while in the introduction to his famous lecture "On Fairy-stories" Tolkien apologizes for being "Overbold", then claims to be "Overbold by name" and "Overbold by nature".

In Tolkien's vivid accounts of battles throughout the Third Age, we discover that many of his cavalry commanders – like Eorl the Young in the Battle of the Field of Celebrant and Théoden in the Battles of the Hornburg and Pelennor Fields – have resorted to Georg von Hohenzollern's *tollkühn* stratagem. It has often turned the tide of battle at its most critical moment, and resulted in many "foolhardy" victories.

THE NORTHMEN OF RHOVANION

Of the Northmen of Rhovanion Tolkien wrote that they were of the "better and nobler sort of Men" who were kin to the Edain of the First Age. They were largely uncorrupted, but in the Third Age remained "in a simple 'Homeric' state of patriarchal and tribal life". They were in fact very like those men celebrated in early Anglo-Saxon epic poetry. The Northmen of Rhovanion (or "Wilderland") were essentially the heroic forebears of Beowulf who made their home for millennia in Europe's trackless forests, mountains and river vales.

Rhovanion was intended to resemble what the ancient Romans called Germania: the great northern forest of Europe. Tolkien also gives them a wild eastern frontier comparable to the Russian steppes. And just as the Roman Empire and its Germanic allies faced wave after wave of Hun, Tartar and Mongol invaders, so the Dúnedain of Gondor and their Northmen allies faced the recurring hostile attacks of the Easterling Balchoth and Variag invaders.

Although most historians have traditionally viewed the early part of the first millennium CE as being dominated by the decline and fall of Rome, a few have seen the period more positively, as a time of change and renewal as vital and active peoples flooded into a weakened, if still-revered, empire. No invading nation wished to bring about the empire's fall. Indeed, even its most barbaric conquerors believed that the Roman Empire would never be destroyed. In one form or another, it had existed for more than a thousand years. The men from the north saw themselves as simply part of another evolution of the empire, in the form of an even greater and revitalized German-Roman state.

In the Northmen of Rhovanion we see something of the

Germanic tribes during the earliest stages of their migrations. They were a noble people who did not greatly diminish the forest or plough up the plains – rural people settled in only a few large towns and scattered villages. They dwelt in the forests, hills and vales of Rhovanion. Among the many tribes and races dwelling in Rhovanion were those later known as the Beornings and Woodmen of Mirkwood, as well as the Bardings and the Men of Dale. However, one other tribe that Tolkien "discovered" in the Vales of Anduin became a particular favourite. These fictional people were called the Éothéod and were linked in Tolkien's mind to the historic Germanic nation of horsemen known as the Goths.

THE KINGS OF ROHAN

Tolkien was fascinated by the Goths. His study of Joseph Wright's *Grammar of the Gothic Language* (1910) was a critical event in his intellectual life. In Gothic, Tolkien observed the first recorded language of the Germanic people and the first recorded language spoken by the progenitors of the English people. Tolkien believed that, through his study of the language and the surviving fragments of Gothic texts, he would gain new insights into this elusive people.

The Goths were Tolkien's inspiration for the Éothéod

(meaning "horse people"), the Rhovanion tribal ancestors of the Riders of Rohan and Lords of the Mark. Both had legendary dragon-slaying forebears: the Éothéod claimed Fram the son of Frumgar as slayer of Scatha the Worm in the Grey Mountains, while the Goths boasted of Wolfdietrich as slayer of the twin dragons of Lombardy.

Tolkien's Éothéod, in alliance with the Kingdom of Gondor, have a story comparable to that of the Goths in alliance with the Empire of Rome. In 451 CE the Goth cavalry carried out a dramatic rescue of the Roman Empire in the Battle of the Catalaunian Fields. This proved to be one of the most critical battles in European history, as the invader was Attila the Hun, the most formidable barbarian force the Romans had ever faced. In T.A. 2050, the forces of Gondor are about to be overrun by barbarian Easterling invaders known as the Balchoth. The Éothéod cavalry of Eorl the Young comes at the critical moment to the Battle of the Field of Celebrant, crushes and destroys the Easterling forces and drives them back to their own lands.

After the Battle of the Catalaunian Fields and the retreat of the invading Huns, as reward for their military service, the Goths became the main inheritors of the lands devastated by the barbarian wars and plagues. Similarly, after the Battle of the Field of Celebrant and the retreat of the Balchoth, as reward for their military service the Éothéod become the main inheritors of the lands devastated by those same factors. This was the fief of

Gondor, previously called Calenardhon, that now became known as Rohan, meaning "Land of the Horse Lords". In these lands, the Horse Lords of Rohan were able to live as free men under their own kings and laws, though always in alliance with Gondor.

Eorl the Young, first king of Rohan

The historic King Theodoric the Goth in the Battle of the Catalaunian Fields inspired Tolkien's account not only of the Battle of the Field of Celebrant led by Eorl, the first king of Rohan, but also the cavalry charge in the Battle of Pelennor Fields led by Théoden, the seventeenth king of Rohan, a thousand years later. Not only were the kings' names almost identical (both meaning "leader of the people" or "king"), but also their victories came at the cost of their own lives, with both kings crushed beneath their fallen steeds.

Throughout the last millennium of the Third Age, the Horsemen of Rohan are the supreme cavalrymen of Middle-earth. Like the historic Goth cavalrymen on the plains east and north of the Western and Eastern Roman Empires, the Rohirrim command the plains of Rohan, and defend the passes into the kingdoms of Arnor and Gondor. The Rohirrim, like the Goths, are constantly armed and prepared for battle, and have a fiery but noble temperament. In fact, Tolkien's descriptions of Rohirric battle tactics were largely based on historic Roman accounts of the Goth and Lombard cavalries.

ESTABLISHMENT OF ROHAN: T.A. 2510 — KINGS OF ROHAN

EVENTS OF THE TIME

Kings	Events of the Time
Eorl the Young *First King* d. T.A. 2545	BATTLE OF THE FIELD OF CELEBRANT T.A. 2510
↓	
Brego *Second King* d. T.A. 2549	BUILDING OF MEDUSELD
↓	
Helm Hammerhand *Ninth King* d. T.A. 2759	BUILDING OF HELM'S DIKE DUNLENDING WARS
↓	
Fréaláf *Tenth King* d. T.A. 2798	SARUMAN TAKES POSSESSION OF ISENGARD
↓	
Brytta *Eleventh King* d. T.A. 2842	ORC WARS
⋮	
Folcwine *Fourteenth King* d. T.A. 2903	BATTLE OF ITHILIEN
⋮	
Thengel *Sixteenth King* d. T.A. 2980	SAURON ENTERS MORDOR

Théoden *Seventeenth King* d. T.A. 3019 — **Théodwyn** d. T.A. 3002

WAR OF THE RING

Théodred d. T.A. 3019

Éomer d. F.A. 63

Éowyn d. F.A. CIRCA 80

LORDS OF THE MARK

A lthough the Riders of Rohan have much history in common with the Goths, Tolkien depicts them in a way almost entirely akin to the ancient Anglo-Saxons – except for the overwhelming significance of the horse in their culture. Essentially, in the Rohirrim we have Beowulf's people plus horses. Indeed, the language of the Rohirrim as "translated" in Tolkien's writings is almost entirely Anglo-Saxon (Old English).

The Rohirrim were also known as the "Riders of the Mark". The term "mark" or "march" meant a borderland and referred to land occupied by an independent ally to serve as a buffer between two hostile nations. Famously, the Franks of Charlemagne set up the Dane Mark (Denmark) as a buffer between themselves and the pagan nations of Scandinavia. In Britain, the Romans established the Welsh Marches, which the Anglo-Saxons called the Mark or the Mearc. This became the kingdom of Mercia that, during the age of Charlemagne, grew into the most powerful kingdom in Britain. This was the heartland of England that Tolkien believed was for centuries the homeland of his mother's Mercian ancestors. It seems likely that in Offa of Mercia (reigned 757–796), the region's most powerful king and the builder of Offa's Dike, Tolkien found considerable inspiration for the ninth king of Rohan, Helm Hammerhand, the builder and defender of the Hornburg – and Helm's Dike.

Humphrey Carpenter, in his biography of Tolkien, notes that, during the period in which he was writing *The Lord of the Rings*, Tolkien took his family on a holiday outing to White Horse Hill, less than twenty miles from Oxford on the borders of Mercia and Wessex. This is the site of the famous prehistoric image of the gigantic White Horse cut into the chalk beneath the green turf and topsoil on the hill. There is no doubt that this landmark that gave Tolkien the image of a white horse on a green field that graces the banners of the kings of Rohan and the Lords of the Mark.

DURIN AND THE SEVEN FATHERS OF THE DWARVES

Tolkien's histories of the Dwarves of Middle-earth are largely those concerning the Dwarves of Durin's Folk. The name "Durin" (or "Durinn") was first recorded in the Icelandic *Prose Edda*, in the "Dvergatal", or "Dwarf's Roll". The name translates as "The Sleeper" or "Sleepy" and is the key to Tolkien's creation story of the "Seven Sleepers". For Tolkien names Durin as the first of the "Seven Fathers of the Dwarves", and as the founder of that greatest Dwarf kingdom, Khazad-dûm (Moria), in the Misty Mountains in the Ages of the Stars.

The Seven Fathers of the Dwarves, Tolkien tells us, are conceived and shaped by Aulë, the Smith of the Valar. It is Aulë, whom the Dwarves call Mahar (meaning "The Maker"), who fashions Dwarves from the substances of the deep earth. From Aulë comes the desire to search down into the roots of mountains, a search to discover the brightest of metals and the most beautiful jewels of the earth. And from Aulë also comes the desire to master crafts such as the carving of stone, the forging of metal and the cutting of gemstones. In their wrathful and violent nature, however, the Dwarves often appear to have more in common with the followers of the warrior cult of Thor, the Norse god of thunder. Unlike the smith gods Hephaestus and Aulë, Thor found glory in battle and honour in the hoarding of gold won by virtue of his war hammer, the Dwarf-forged thunderbolt.

In their conception, Aulë's Seven Fathers of the Dwarves are in many ways similar to the creatures conceived by the smith god of the Greeks, Hephaestus. These appeared to be living creatures, but in fact were robot-like automatons designed to help him in his smithy to beat metal and work the forges. The original Seven Fathers of the Dwarves are in the beginning, like those automatons, incapable of independent thought or life. They can move only on command or by the thought of their master. It is Ilúvatar who gives the Dwarves the gift of true life, although he does not permit them to walk upon Middle-earth before the awakening of his own creations, the Elves. Hence the Seven

Opposite: Durin's folk in battle formation

Fathers of the Dwarves sleep through the ages until the dark skies are filled with starlight by Varda, the Star Queen.

There can be little doubt of Tolkien's intentions here, for one of the many names for the Star Queen is the High Elvish Fanuilos, which translates as "Snow White". This is somewhat disorienting. Having just got used to the revelation that the "Seven Dwarves" were the real "Sleepers" in Tolkien's version of the Snow White and the Seven Dwarfs fairy tale, we now discover that it is Snow White who is actually responsible for the awakening of the Seven Dwarves.

In the history of the Dwarves in the Third Age, a terrible fate befalls Durin's Folk in T.A. 1980 when, in delving deep in the mines of Khazad-dûm, the Dwarves awake a monstrous demon of fire. This is an ancient Maia fire spirit known as a Balrog or Valaraukar, meaning "demon of might". The source of Tolkien's inspiration for this gigantic monster is the Norse fire giant Surt – meaning "the Black One" – who was the Lord of Muspelheim, the evil volcanic underworld of the Norse fire giants. In Norse mythology, Surt – armed with his flaming sword – will fight the Norse gods and set their world on fire in the final battle of Ragnarök. In Middle-earth, the Balrog with his flaming sword and "scourges of fire" slew King Durin VI and drove Durin's folk from Khazad-dûm.

For the final thousand years of the Third Age, Khazad-dûm ("Dwarf-Mansion") is known as "Moria" ("Black Chasm") and remains a place of terror comparable to Surt's Muspelheim. It is an evil realm of fire and darkness inhabited by Orcs, Trolls, serpents and unnamed monsters. This marks the beginning of the diaspora of Durin's Folk. Driven from their ancient kingdom, they are constantly on the move, exiles in search of a safe new realm. But in the Third Age the terrors that lurk in the scattered realms of Durin's Folk also endanger the kingdoms of the Dúnedain. The Balrog in Moria, Orcs in the Misty Mountains and Dragons in the Grey Mountains and Erebor not only threaten the Dwarves of Durin's Folk, but all the Free Peoples of Middle-earth. And so, in the Dúnedain of Arnor and Gondor, Durin's Dwarves find natural allies.

Woses, allies of the Rohirrim and Dúnedain in the Siege of Gondor

Furthermore, the messianism found among the Dúnedain (in their tradition of an eventual "return of the king") is even more prevalent among the Dwarves. Durin I is known as "Durin the Deathless" only in part because he was very long-lived. More significantly, he is considered "deathless" because, not unlike real-world spiritual leaders, the Dwarves believe that each king who carries the name Durin is actually a reincarnation of the original Father of the Dwarves. It is a mysterious cycle spanning many millennia, ending only with the seventh and final incarnation, Durin VII.

The Corsairs of Umbar, the chief enemies of the Dúnedain of Gondor

LONGBEARDS — DWARVES OF DURIN'S LINE

EVENTS OF THE TIME

Durin's Line	Events of the Time	
Durin I *Khazad-dûm*	AGES OF THE STARS	
Durin III *Moria*	S.A. 1695–1701 WAR OF ELVES AND SAURON	
Durin IV *Moria*	S.A. 3434–3441 LAST ALLIANCE OF ELVES AND MEN	
Durin VI *Moria*	T.A. 1980–3019 BALROG IN MORIA	
Náin II *Grey Mountains*	T.A. 2570 DRAGONS IN NORTH	
Dáin I *Grey Mountains*	T.A. 2589 COLD DRAKES IN GREY MTS.	**Borin** *Erebor*
Thrór *Erebor*	T.A. 2770–2942 SMAUG THE DRAGON IN EREBOR	**Farin** *(Exile)*
Thráin II *(Exile)*	T.A. 2793–2799 WAR OF DWARVES AND ORCS	**Gróin** *(Exile)*
Thorin II Oakenshield *Exile/Erebor*	T.A. 2941 BATTLE OF FIVE ARMIES	**Glóin** *(Exile/Erebor)*
Dáin II Ironfoot *Iron Hills/Erebor*	T.A. 3019 WAR OF THE RING	**Gimli Elf-friend** *Erebor/Aglarond*
Thorin III Stonehelm *Erebor*		
Durin VII the Last		

PART
SIX

HEROES OF THE THIRD AGE: PART II. HOBBITS AND DWARVES

ORIGIN OF THE HOBBIT

I n a hole in the ground there lived a hobbit." One of the best-known opening lines in the history of literature, this sentence told the world of the existence of Hobbits. It was also the world's introduction to the first Hobbit hero, Bilbo Baggins of Bag End.

The Hobbit was published in 1937 and rapidly established itself as a children's classic. Curiously, we actually know exactly where and how the first Hobbit appeared in his creator's mind. On a warm summer afternoon in 1930, J. R. R. Tolkien was sitting at his desk in his study at 20 Northmoor Road in the suburbs of Oxford. He was engaged in the "everlasting weariness" of marking School Certificate papers, when "on a blank leaf I scrawled 'In a hole in the ground there lived a hobbit.' I did not and do not know why."

Tolkien was a professor of Anglo-Saxon and a philologist (a scholar who studies words and their origins). He had worked as a scholar on the *Oxford English Dictionary* and knew the English language (and many other languages) to its very roots. So when Tolkien later spoke of that moment when the word "hobbit" first came to him, he commented: "Names always generate a story in my mind. Eventually I thought I'd better find out what hobbits were like. But that was only a beginning." Indeed, "only a beginning" is a profound understatement.

Tolkien really did start with the word "hobbit". It became a kind of riddle that needed solving. He decided that he must begin by inventing a philological origin for the word as a worn-down form of an original invented word *holbytla* (which is actually an Anglo-Saxon or Old English construct), meaning "hole builder". Therefore the opening line of the novel is an obscure lexicographical joke and a weird piece of circular thinking: "In a hole in the ground there lived a hole builder."

Tolkien, not content to joke in just one invented language, extends this to a series of philological puns on "hole" and "hole builder" in Old English, Old German (*hohl*), and an invented "Hobbitish" speech (*khuduk*) based on constructs from Gothic ("*kud-dukan*") and prehistoric German ("*khulaz*") words. (In later years, he would invent two variations in his Elvish

Elrond Half-elven's Rivendell home

languages, another one in the language of the Dwarves, and several in the Mannish tongues.)

This is an unusual way to develop a character and write a novel, but it was clearly an essential part of Tolkien's creative process. Nearly all aspects of Hobbit life and adventure seem to evolve from names for people and things. Tolkien believed names resonate with the force of their legends: words that name or describe dragons or demons often carry force over the human imagination even if their history is unknown and their tale untold.

Tolkien's Hobbits, naturally enough, relate to the traditions of the land itself. Hobbits are derived, in part, from the mythology of the ancient Britons (a Proto-Welsh-speaking people) who were among the earliest inhabitants of Britain. These are the Celtic sprites of the untamed British hills and forests – the brownies – who were commonly known as hobs, hob men, hob thrusts and hob hursts. These sprites were a diminutive, hairy, elusive race, mostly friendly towards humans. Brownies measured two to three feet in height and hid themselves away in the "hollow hills" (usually ancient grave mounds or barrow tombs) of the wild Celtic landscape.

It seems we do not have to look very far for direct inspiration for Tolkien's race of hole-dwelling little people. Hobs and hob men were frequently called the "people of the hills". Tolkien certainly knew a great deal about the tales and traditions of the

Celtic brownies. Indeed, only a few miles from Tolkien's Oxford home, there is an ancient round barrow tomb still known as Hob Hurst's House. Hobs and Tolkien's Hobbits are, however, two very distinct races in nature and purpose. What Tolkien gives us in his tea-drinking, pipe-smoking, home-and-garden-oriented Hobbits is a distinctively English transmutation of those wild and anything-but-middle-class hobs and hob men of the Celts.

In fact, Tolkien's Hobbits are a distillation of all that is fundamentally "English", regardless of era. The anachronistic mix of the genteel "cakes and tea" manners of the late Victorians and the tribal traditions of the ancient Anglo-Saxons is intentional and meant to be gently satirical. At the same time, there is a serious intent on Tolkien's part to create in his Hobbits a race that embodies the enduring spirit of that ideal "little England" characterized by the lands and villages of the English shires.

The homeland of the Hobbits of Middle-earth is the tilled fields and farmlands of the Shire. This is J. R. R. Tolkien's romanticized analogy for the rural landscapes of his

Bilbo Baggins

Bag End, home of Bilbo Baggins

late-Victorian childhood, as yet barely touched by the ravages of the Industrial Revolution. His Hobbits are the yeomen of England's "green and pleasant land". They are to the tilled fields and rolling farmlands what Dwarves are to the mountains: the genii, or guardian spirits, of the place.

"The Shire is based on rural England and not any other country in the world," Tolkien once wrote. It was also "a parody of rural England, in much the same sense as are its inhabitants: they go together and are meant to. After all the book is English, and by an Englishman."

BILBO BAGGINS OF BAG END

The first and original Hobbit created by J. R. R. Tolkien was a certain gentlehobbit by the name of Bilbo Baggins. We have examined the word "hobbit" and observed what that word contributed to the race. Now let us examine the given names of the quintessential Hobbit, Bilbo, and see what they contribute to his individual character.

Let us begin with the surname: Baggins can be related to a Middle English Somerset surname, Bagg, meaning "money-bag" or "wealthy", while "baggins" is a Lancashire dialect word for "afternoon tea or snack between meals". Certainly, Baggins is an appropriate family name for a prosperous and well-fed Hobbit. Superficially and initially, Bilbo Baggins is presented as a mildly comic, home-loving, rustic, middle-class gentlehobbit. He is harmless and obsequious, full of gossip, homely wisdom, wordy euphemisms and elaborate family histories. He is largely concerned with home comforts, village fetes, dinner parties, flower gardens, vegetable plots and grain harvests.

Bilbo Baggins is a comic anti-hero who goes off on a journey into a heroic world. It is a world where the commonplace knocks up against the heroic. Values are different in these worlds. In Bilbo Baggins we have a character with modern everyday sensibilities whom the reader may identify with but who has an adventure in an ancient heroic world.

Another aspect of Bilbo Baggins's character is revealed by an analysis of his first name. The word "bilbo" entered the English language in the fifteenth century and probably derives from the Basque city of Bilbao, once renowned for the making of delicate swords of flexible, but almost unbreakable, steel. In Shakespearean times, a bilbo was a short but deadly piercing sword – a small thrusting rapier.

This is an excellent description of Bilbo's sword, the charmed Elf knife called Sting. Found in a Troll hoard, Bilbo's bilbo is an Elven blade that can pierce through armour or animal hide that would break any other sword. In *The Hobbit*, however, it is our hero's sharp wit rather than his sharp sword that gives Bilbo the edge. Whether he's escaping from Orcs, Elves, Gollum or the Dragon, Bilbo's sharp wit allows him to solve riddles and trick villains.

When we put the two names together as Bilbo Baggins, we have two aspects of our hero's character, and to some degree the character of Hobbits in general. On the face of it, the name Baggins suggests a harmless, well-to-do, contented character, while the name Bilbo suggests an individual who is sharp, intelligent and even a little dangerous.

GANDALF THE WIZARD

G andalf the Wizard appears in *The Hobbit* as a standard fairy-tale character: a rather comic, eccentric magician in the company of a band of Dwarves. He has something of the character of the absent-minded history professor and muddled conjurer about him. Gandalf also fulfils the traditional role of mentor, adviser and tour guide for the hero (or anti-hero) of the story. Wizards are extremely useful and versatile as vehicles for developing fairy-tale plots, as their presence in so many tales testifies. Wizards usually provide a narrative with: a reluctant hero, secret maps, translations of ancient documents, supernatural weapons (how to use), some monsters (how to kill), location of treasure (how to steal) and an escape plan (negotiable).

Gandalf the Grey certainly fits into this tradition of the fairy tale. It is Gandalf who brings the Dwarves and the Hobbit together at the start of the story and sets them on their quest. It is his injection of adventure and magic into the mundane world of the Hobbits that transforms Bilbo Baggins's life. It is Gandalf who leads the band of outlaw adventurers, Thorin and Company, to Bilbo's door. And it is just this combination of the everyday and the epic that makes *The Hobbit* so compelling. Grand adventures with dragons, trolls, elves and treasure are combined

Opposite: Gandalf the Grey in the Shire

with afternoon teas, toasted muffins, pints of ale and smoke-ring-blowing contests.

So, in *The Hobbit*, Gandalf is a fairy-tale magician with a traditional pointy hat, long cape and wizard's staff. He is an amusing and reassuring presence, like a fairy godfather. His later transformation in *The Lord of the Rings* is something of a surprise, but then Tolkien is making the point that behind all fairy-tale magicians there are powerful archetypes from the myths and epics of a racial past.

The sources of Gandalf are many: Merlin of the Britons, Odin of the Norsemen, Wotan of the ancient Germans, Mercury of the Romans, Hermes of the Greeks and Thoth of the Egyptians. All are linked with magic, sorcery, arcane knowledge and secret doctrine. Most obviously, Gandalf, Merlin, Odin and Wotan all commonly took on the form of a wandering old man in a grey cloak carrying a staff. Gandalf was comparable to the others in powers and deeds as well. Typically, these wizards served as guides and frequently used their supernatural powers to help heroes advance against impossible odds.

WIZARDS AND WANDERING GODS

The most common portrayal of the wizard is that of a solitary wanderer wearing a broad-brimmed hat and a long traveller's cape, and bearing a long staff. Traditionally, these wanderers tend to be bearded and world-weary individuals of distant or unknown origin. They are often mesmerizing when it comes to the telling of tales and recitation of literature, but they are "outsiders". They do not appear to have any personal wealth or material support; they do not have definable status or social position; nor do they have families or homes. Literate in many languages and customs, these solitary wanderers are widely believed to be capable of casting spells and curses, and of acts of sorcery.

What is seldom observed about the wizard's garb is that it was the same costume worn by nearly all pilgrims and professional travellers in antiquity. There were once many peripatetic professions and activities – travelling scholars, pilgrims, traders, merchants, scribes, surveyors, musicians, conjurers and apothecaries – all of whom dressed in similar garb. There were also professional messengers, couriers and diplomatic envoys who were continuously on the road, and they wore stylized "uniform" versions of the same or a similar costume. This was probably because it was the combination of clothing that was best suited to travelling in all weathers.

It is also how the Greek god Hermes (and the Roman Mercury) was portrayed in his guise as the god of travellers. Hermes was the swift messenger of the Olympians, and a pillar featuring this bearded god of travellers appeared at most crossroads. Hermes, like his fellow god Odin, frequently appeared on earth as an ordinary traveller where both civic law and popular superstition supported the traditions of hospitality. For, as any traveller might be a god in disguise, all travellers should be treated with equal respect and honour.

It therefore did no harm to a poor pilgrim to somewhat resemble this god of travellers, who was also the god of magicians, alchemists, merchants, pilgrims, scholars, messengers, envoys, diplomats and – predictably – liars and thieves. As the herald of the gods, Hermes (or Mercury) passes through all the domains of the other gods: from Olympus, the realm of Zeus (or Jupiter), where he is the herald of the gods, to the underworld, the kingdom of Hades (or Pluto), where he guides the souls of the dead.

It may be supposed that, when the ancients decided to assign gods and their influences to the planets, Mercury as the grey wanderer (and speeding messenger) must have been one of their more obvious choices. After all, the word "planet" is derived from the Greek word "wanderer". (As most stars are "fixed" in the sky, the most obvious quality of a planet is its ability to wander through the night sky, hence the use of this word for this particular meaning.) Mercury is observably a silver-grey "wanderer" travelling at phenomenal speed across the night sky, visiting each god or planet, as paths cross. There could be no clearer case for matching up the mercurial nature of both the planet and the god.

Thorin and Company at the door to the Lonely Mountain

THORIN AND COMPANY

he quiet life of Bilbo Baggins of Bag End is forever disturbed by the unexpected arrival of thirteen Dwarves. Known as Thorin and Company, these conspirators – aided

and abetted by the Gandalf the Wizard – recruit the respectable Hobbit as a specialist burglar and entice him into joining in their adventure through Wilderland.

As Tolkien's intention in *The Hobbit* was to deliberately write an adventure novel for children, the initial portrayal of the Dwarves of Thorin and Company is largely consistent with the rather comic fairy-tale dwarfs of Snow White. However, the reader does get glimpses of the long tragic history of the Dwarves that inform the stubborn (and ultimately heroic) character of Thorin Oakenshield through his accounts of wars, feuds and battles in ages long gone by. Something of the ancient heritage of the Dwarves is also conveyed in their names.

Where do these names originate? Tolkien took the names directly from the primary source of Viking mythology: Iceland's twelfth-century text the *Prose Edda*. The *Edda* suggests a crude account of the creation of the Dwarfs, and then lists their names; this list is usually called the *Dvergatal*, or the "Dwarf's Roll". All the Dwarves in *The Hobbit* appear in this list: Thorin, Dwalin, Balin, Kíli, Fíli, Bifur, Bofur, Bombur, Dori, Nori, Ori, Óin and Glóin. Other names of Dwarves which Tolkien found in the *Edda*, and used later, include Thráin, Thrór, Dáin and Náin.

Not surprisingly, the name of the leader of the Tolkien's Company of Adventurers is Thorin, which means "bold". However, Tolkien also gave him another Dwarf-name from the list: Eikinskjaldi, meaning "he of the Oakenshield". This name

Opposite: Thorin Oakenshield and Company

provoked Tolkien into inventing a complex piece of background history wherein, during a battle in the Goblin Wars, Thorin broke his sword but fought on by picking up an oak bough that he used as both a club and a shield.

Thráin, meaning "stubborn", was the name of Thorin's father, who was slain by Dragons when he stubbornly resisted the Dragon's invasion of his realm. Thorin's sister was Dís, which simply means "sister". Thorin's heir and avenger, who led the Dwarves of Iron Mountain, Dáin Ironfoot or "Deadly Ironfoot", proved to be true to his warrior name.

The names of other members of the Company were instrumental in Tolkien's shaping of their character. Bombur, meaning "bulging", is certainly the fattest of the Dwarves, and Nori, meaning "peewee", is the smallest; Balin, meaning "burning one", is fiery in battle, but warm with his friends; Ori, meaning "furious", fought furiously before he is slain in Moria; and Glóin, meaning "glowing one", wins glory and riches.

There seems little doubt that the *Dvergatal* list of names was a rich source of inspiration for Tolkien and the means by which he "discovered" the character of his Dwarves.

Thorin Oakenshield

DWARVES OF THORIN AND COMPANY

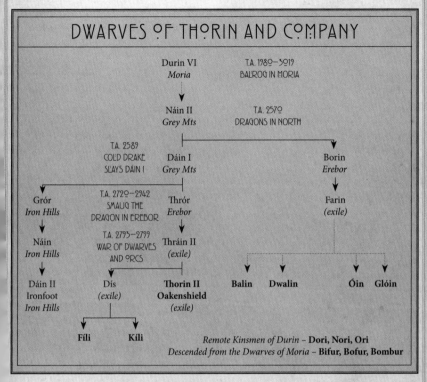

Durin VI
Moria

T.A. 1980–3019
BALROG IN MORIA

Náin II
Grey Mts

T.A. 2570
DRAGONS IN NORTH

T.A. 2589
COLD DRAKE
SLAYS DÁIN I

Dáin I
Grey Mts

Borin
Erebor

Grór
Iron Hills

T.A. 2770–2942
SMAUG THE
DRAGON IN EREBOR

Thrór
Erebor

Farin
(exile)

Náin
Iron Hills

T.A. 2793–2799
WAR OF DWARVES
AND ORCS

Thráin II
(exile)

Dáin II
Ironfoot
Iron Hills

Dís
(exile)

Thorin II
Oakenshield
(exile)

Balin   Dwalin   Óin   Glóin

Fíli   Kíli

Remote Kinsmen of Durin – **Dori, Nori, Ori**
Descended from the Dwarves of Moria – **Bifur, Bofur, Bombur**

BILBO BAGGINS THE BURGLAR

A s Tolkien implied in Bilbo Baggins's name, there is always something different and contrary in Bilbo Baggins's nature: he is a typical Hobbit, full of practical common sense, but also sharp-witted and very un-Hobbitish in his curiosity about the wider world. He is chosen, on one level, Tolkien explains, as the "lucky number fourteen" to avoid the unlucky number of thirteen adventurers in Thorin's Company. But, most obviously, Bilbo is chosen for the job of master burglar because of his stealth, as Hobbits possessed a natural ability to move about quietly and unnoticed by larger folk.

In the everyday world, a burglar is a criminal shunned by society; in the world of fairy tale and myth, the burglar is a celebrated hero whose skill, wit and bravery are celebrated and whose deeds result in the enrichment of his whole family, tribe and people. This is typical of many fairy-tale plots, such as "Jack and the Beanstalk" or indeed many of the world's myths where the hero travels to another realm and steals treasure, magical weapons or even the secret of making fire.

Why do Gandalf and Thorin think Bilbo Baggins will make a good burglar to assist the Dwarves in the theft of the Dragon's treasure? The answer appears to come in Tolkien's own statement: "Names always generate a story in my mind." Once again, Tolkien was indulging in wordplay: Bilbo Baggins was a burgher who became a burglar. Tom Shippley, in *The Road to Middle-earth*, explores this idea in his chapter "The Bourgeois Burglar". A burgher, he observes, was a freeman of a burgh or borough (or a burrow), and this certainly applies to Bilbo Baggins. Even more, its derivative, *bourgeois*, describes a person with humdrum middle-class ideas. The Germanic cognate word *burg* means "mound, fort, stockaded house".

A burgher is one who owns a house; a burglar is one who plunders a house. So, we have the everyday humdrum middle-class burgher entering a fairy-tale world and being transformed into his opposite – a burglar.

THE QUEST OF EREBOR:
THE LONELY MOUNTAIN

As the Quest of Erebor begins, despite Gandalf's reassurances to Thorin and Company, Bilbo Baggins appears to be totally incompetent as a mercenary burglar. Indeed, Bilbo has to be shamed into accepting the role as master burglar or thief. And first time out, the Hobbit leads all thirteen Dwarves to near-disaster when he is captured by three very slow-witted Trolls in the Trollshaws (literally "troll-woods").

The encounter with the Trolls is rather imitative of the Brothers Grimm tale "The Brave Little Tailor", as well as of trickster tales from Icelandic mythology. However, it is the wizard Gandalf who, like the Tailor, uses his wits to keep the Trolls quarrelling until the sun rises and turns these creatures of darkness to stone. It is a plot line common to fairy tales about outsmarting trolls, giants and other monsters. The narrator's note that "Trolls ... must be underground before dawn" is a folk belief that likely goes back long before the twelfth century when it was recorded in the Icelandic poem "Alvíssmál" in the *Prose Edda*.

In this episode, Gandalf provides Bilbo Baggins with his first lesson in using his wits to outsmart larger and more powerful foes. And, as is typical in such fairy tales, the hero's reward is a treasure hoard and the acquisition of weapons that become essential in the adventures ahead, in this instance, three Elven blades – one sword each for Gandalf and Thorin, and one dagger that serves well enough as a sword for a Hobbit.

MASTER ELROND HALF-ELVEN

Leaving the Trollshaws behind, Gandalf leads Thorin and Company into the hidden valley of Rivendell and the domain of Master Elrond the Half-elven. Considered the "Last Homely House East of the Sea", for four thousand years Rivendell has been a refuge of wisdom and great learning for all Elves and Men of goodwill.

Tolkien described the north-west of Middle-earth as being geographically equivalent to Europe and the north shore of the Mediterranean, famously stating that "Hobbiton and Rivendell are taken ... to be at about the latitude of Oxford". However, it is quite apparent that Rivendell is not just "on the latitude of Oxford"; it is an analogue for Oxford itself.

In Rivendell, the common tongue was Westron, while the

true scholar's choice was the ancient Elvish languages of Sindarin and Quenya. In Oxford, the common tongue was English, while the true scholar's choice was the ancient languages of Latin and Greek. In Tolkien's mind, Rivendell was an Elvish Oxford, and Oxford through two world wars was an English Rivendell: a refuge of wisdom and great learning where scribes and scholars might work in peace in the midst of a world gone mad with the slaughter of war.

Master Elrond's use of language was somewhat archaic, but not excessively so for someone who is essentially a six-thousand-year-old embodiment of Oxford's Ashmolean Institute and Bodleian Library combined. *The Silmarillion* reveals much of Elrond's Half-elven heritage, but in *The Hobbit* he wears his wisdom lightly, and we are simply told: "Elrond knew all about runes of every kind." He serves as a kind of oracle, common in myth and legend, providing the ancient lore essential for the progress of questing heroes.

In Tolkien's world, entry into most of his Dwarf kingdoms is made through secret doors in mountain walls. As with most fairy tales containing the door-in-the-mountain motif, these doors lead to the discovery of a lost inheritance or a cursed hoard of gold, and require the intelligence of the hero to outwit or pacify the guardians of these treasures within the mountains. Entry is commonly achieved by means of a spell, a golden key or the answer to some kind of riddle. These vary from the "Open

Sesame!" of "Ali Baba and the Forty Thieves", to the magic ring
of "Aladdin", to the musical tune that commands the stone doors
in the tale "The Pied Piper of Hamelin". In *The Hobbit*, entry
into the Kingdom under the Mountain through the secret door
proves to be complicated. Gandalf has obtained a map and a key,
but even so it requires the wisdom of Elrond Half-elven to read
hidden "moon-letters" that reveal clues to the exact time, place
and means by which the door-in-the-mountain of Erebor may be
discovered and opened.

GOLLUM AND THE GOBLINS

In attempting to cross over a high pass through the Misty
Mountains, Bilbo Baggins and Thorin and Company become
entrapped in the subterranean kingdom of Goblin Town.
At one point in the narrative, Tolkien says that the mountains
are infested with "goblins, hobgoblins and orcs of the worst
description". This list is, of course, somewhat redundant, as all
three belong to the same race of nasty creatures. Tolkien's evil,
irredeemable Orcs of *The Silmarillion* are in *The Hobbit* given
the rather more generic name of Goblins to more comfortably fit
into the fairy-tale world of children's literature.

The escape from Goblin Town is achieved in part by Gandalf
and Thorin making good use of their newly acquired Elven

swords – Glamdring, or "Foe-hammer", and Orcrist, or "Goblin-cleaver" – taken from the Trolls' hoard. Meanwhile, although Bilbo's possession of his Elven dagger does offer him some protection from immediate attack by the monstrous would-be cannibal Gollum, it is his wit in answering riddles that sustains him, and his "luck" in the discovery of a magic ring that actually allows him to escape.

As Tolkien once explained, in *The Hobbit*, Bilbo's discovery of the ring of invisibility was essentially "a device" – quite common in the plot of many fairy tales – to transform the everyday individual into an extraordinary hero. However, the true significance and history of the ring – before he began work years later on *The Lord of the Rings* – was no more apparent to the author at that time than it was to the Hobbit. However, Bilbo's finding of the ring on the tunnel floor cannot have been pure chance, as the narrator in *The Hobbit* observes: "It was a turning point in his career, but he did not know it." He uses it to escape Gollum and the Orcs and even to bypass the Dwarves who immediately recognize his stealthy skill and begin to treat him with considerable respect.

With his victory over the wily Gollum and the theft of his ring, Bilbo's apprenticeship to Gandalf the Wizard is complete: "Thief! Thief! Thief! Baggins! We hates it, we hates it for ever!" This is high praise indeed from a veteran fellow criminal who has been stealing and murdering for centuries.

BEORN AND BEOWULF

fter the adventure in Goblin Town, there are a few moments of respite as the party of adventurers is given shelter and sustenance by Beorn, the eponymous chieftain of the Beornings. Beorn is a huge, black-bearded man garbed

Beorn the Skin-changer

in a coarse wool tunic and armed with a woodsman's axe. It is immediately apparent that we are now firmly in the heroic world of the Anglo-Saxons, for Beorn appears to be something approaching the Middle-earth twin brother of the epic hero Beowulf. With his pride in his strength, his code of honour, his terrible wrath and his hospitality, Beorn is Beowulf, transposed and diminished into fairy-tale mode. Even his home seems a small-scale version of Heorot, the mead-hall of King Hrothgar.

In fact, Tolkien, by way of a philological manipulation, gives his character a name that sounds and looks different from Beowulf's, but in the end means much the same. "Beorn" is a keeper of bees and a lover of honey. His name means "man" in Old English; however, in its Norse form, it means "bear". Meanwhile, if we look at the Old English name Beowulf, we discover that it literally and quite strangely means "bee-wolf". What is a bee-wolf? This is typical of the sort of riddle-name the ancient Anglo-Saxons liked to construct. "What wolf hunts bees – and steals their honey?" The answer is obvious enough: "bee-wolf" is a kenning for a bear. Thus, Beowulf and Beorn both mean "bear". One might say that Beowulf and Beorn are the same men with different names, or, in their symbolic guise as bee-wolf and bear, they are the same animal in different skins.

Tolkien presents Beorn as the founder of the Beornings, the "man-bear" people who are closely related to similar man-bear "skin-changers" referred to in Icelandic literature, the bear-cult

warriors known as the "berserkers" – a name derived from "bear-sark" or "bear-shirts". The historical berserkers in "holy battle rage" felt themselves to be possessed by the ferocious spirit of the enraged bear: as Odin's holy warriors, wearing only animal skins, they sometimes charged into battle unarmed, but in such a rage that they tore the enemy limb from limb with their bare hands and teeth. Such states, however, were but a pale imitation of what was the core miracle of the cult: the incarnate transformation of man into bear.

Once again, Tolkien uses a name to inspire his imagination. Soon enough, Beorn the bear-man is revealed as a "skin-changer" with the power of transformation: from man to beast and beast to man. It is a supernatural power that eventually makes Beorn a critical factor in the outcome of the Battle of the Five Armies.

MIRKWOOD AND THE ELVENKING

N ow we come to the most dangerous part of the journey," the narrator informs us as the Hobbit and Thorin and Company march into the great forest of Mirkwood. By the Third Age, Mirkwood has become a place of dread, haunted and infested by Goblins, Wolves and Great Spiders. The very name Mirkwood conveys the sense of superstitious dread of primeval forests found in many of the fairy tales of the Brothers Grimm,

Opposite: Thranduil, King of Woodland Realm

including "Little Red Riding Hood" and "Hansel and Gretel" – as well as in Arthurian legend.

In Germanic and Norse epic poetry, the dark forest is ever present and is even sometimes specifically given the name Mirkwood. In the *Völsunga* saga, Sigurd the Dragon-slayer enters Mirkwood and stops to mourn the loss of the "Glittering Heath", now ruined by the corruption of Fafnir the Dragon. This theme of wilderness contaminated by evil is evident in Tolkien's own spider-infested Mirkwood, and is later repeated in the wasteland known as the Desolation of Smaug, the Dragon of Erebor.

It is in Mirkwood that Bilbo Baggins twice saves the beleaguered Company of Dwarves and really proves his mettle. His transformation is remarkable. In Mirkwood, the timid Bilbo becomes a hero of the most ferocious kind. With his glowing Elf blade Sting and his ring of invisibility, he ruthlessly slaughters the evil Great Spiders of Mirkwood. Then, when the Dwarves are taken captive by the Elvenking, it is Bilbo who engineers their escape from his prison. Thereafter, the Company undertakes a relatively uneventful journey to Lake Town and onward to the Dwarf Kingdom under the Mountain. There, the ultimate test of Bilbo Baggins's skill as a master burglar lies waiting in the lair of the Dragon of the Lonely Mountain.

While the epic tales of *The Silmarillion* are focused on the history of the Elves in which the Dwarves play only a peripheral part, the reverse is the case in *The Hobbit*. Here the Elves are subsidiary, the Wood Elves in particular initially portrayed as generic fairy-tale elves, full of song and good cheer. While Tolkien does give his readers a casual glimpse into the complex and developing mythology of his "Light Elves and the Deep-elves and Sea Elves", here the king of the Mirk has only a title, not a proper name – "Elvenking". His actual name was revealed only in *The Lord of the Rings*, as Thandruil, King of the Woodland Realm (the father of Legolas Greenleaf). And, by tracing his ancestry backward to Beleriand – his father, Oropher, was a Sindarin lord of Doriath – we can deduce that his capital is essentially a scaled-down version of Menegroth, the city of the thousand caves.

Tolkien also gives readers of *The Hobbit* just the slightest glimpse of the origin of the blood feud between Dwarves and Elves. In this Tolkien was inspired by the Norse legend of the theft of the Brisingamen, the "Necklace of the Brising Dwarves", which resulted in an endless war between two kings. In *The Hobbit*, the Elvenking alludes to the theft of the Nauglamír, or "Necklace of the Dwarves", that resulted in a six-thousand-year feud between Elves and Dwarves.

THE GOLDEN DRAGON OF EREBOR

rmed with his ring and Sting, and given confidence
by his adventures in Mirkwood, Bilbo Baggins is
ready for his supreme test as a master burglar. Tolkien
acknowledged that the circumstances and actions of the Hobbit
in this first encounter with the Dragon of Erebor was – at least
subconsciously – inspired by a passage in *Beowulf*. In a letter
to the English newspaper the *Observer* in 1938, Tolkien wrote:
"*Beowulf* is among my most valued sources; though it was
not consciously present to the mind in the process of writing,
in which the episode of the theft arose naturally (and almost
inevitably) from the circumstances."

While the two tales are not overtly similar, there are strong
plot parallels between the dragon episode in *Beowulf* and the
slaying of Smaug in *The Hobbit*. Beowulf's dragon wakes when
a thief finds his way into the creature's cave and steals a jewelled
cup from the treasure hoard. This scenario is duplicated when
Bilbo finds his way into Smaug the Dragon's cavern and steals
a jewelled cup from the treasure hoard. Both thieves avoid
the immediate detection of their crime and the danger of the
dragons themselves; however, the nearby human settlements in
the tales suffer terribly from the dragons' wrath.

As ever, Tolkien plays on names. Smaug, despite his great

Opposite: Bilbo Baggins in the lair of Smaug the Golden

power, is – in common with other dragons of myth and legend – vain and susceptible to flattery, and when Bilbo is caught during his second visit to the hoard, Smaug is easily distracted by the Hobbit's riddles. To be precise: Smaug is smug. His arrogance and contempt for his foes render him liable to succumb to the Hobbit's stratagems, giving Bilbo the chance to discover Smaug's "Achilles' heel". In a long tradition of dragon lore that extends at least as far back as Fafnir the Dragon of the *Völsunga* saga, the secret of a great serpent's soft underbelly was a well-established one – and not actually much of a secret. However, Smaug has taken the precaution of protecting himself with a "diamond waistcoat" of embedded jewels. The Hobbit's delaying tactics give him the opportunity to observe a single bare patch in the jewelled carapace. It is this information – passed on by a thrush – that Bard the Bowman of Lake-town is later able to use to finally destroy the "great worm".

BATTLE OF THE FIVE ARMIES

The death of Smaug does not end the quest, of course, but instead unleashes an apocalyptic battle between the opposing forces of good and evil as they compete for control of Erebor and its treasures. The spectacular Battle of the Five Armies is an example of "eucastrophe", a catastrophe that has a sudden turn and results in a happy ending. It was a word coined by Tolkien himself in his landmark essay "On Fairy Stories". "Eucastrophe" is a Greek construct that strictly translates as a "good destruction". This, Tolkien argued, was "the true form of fairy-tale and its highest function". He observed that, while tragedy was the true form of drama, the consolation of a happy ending was essential for the fairy-story – no matter how frightening or terrifying the preceding adventures.

In the Battle of the Five Armies, the heroes of the quest come together under the banners of the Wood-elves, the Men of Lake-town and Dale, and the Dwarves of Erebor and the Iron Mountains, in an uneven conflict with the overwhelming hordes of Goblins of Dol Guldur and Gundabad, and the Wargs (wild wolves) of Mirkwood (the precise identification of the two evil armies varies). On the fairy-tale scale of *The Hobbit*, this is a battle of epic proportions, even if in the larger context of the many wars of Middle-earth, it might appear somewhat less cataclysmic.

The odds are stacked against the armies of the Dwarves, Men and Elves, who are outnumbered ten to one by the hordes of Goblins, Wolves and Wolf-riders. So, despite the fierce resolve of Thranduil's Elves and Bard's Men, and despite the brave sacrifice of the Dwarves in Thorin Oakenshield's last charge into the fray, the forces of the free people are on the brink of annihilation. At that critical moment, Tolkien gives his heroes their moment of deliverance. This was Tolkien's eucastrophe – "a sudden and

miraculous grace". A host of Great Eagles of the Misty Mountains arrives like the cavalry, joined a little later by Beorn in the form of a huge "were-bear". Virtually invulnerable to weapons and filled with battle rage, Beorn brings terror onto the battlefield, while the Eagles descend on the Goblins like deadly lightning bolts. These supernatural interventions are what Classical scholars call a deus ex machina – the reversal of disaster at the end of a play by the timely intervention of a deity – Tolkien's Eagles taking the place of Zeus/Jupiter, who sometimes took eagle form. And so, the tide of the Battle of the Five Armies is turned, and the forces of evil overthrown.

Gwaihir the Windlord and the Eagles of Misty Mountains

FROM HOBBIT TO HERO

"I came from the end of a bag, but no bag went over me," riddles Bilbo Baggins of Bag End in his contest of wits with the Dragon of Erebor. The Hobbit and his creator are fascinated with puns, word games and riddles, and – by a certain literary sleight of hand – we have been entertained by the story of an everyday bourgeois transformed into a daring burglar.

Another perspective on the transformation of Bilbo Baggins can be gained from observing exactly what kind of burglar the Hobbit becomes. This may be determined by conjuring up a closely associated word and profession – the "hobbler". In Britain, "hobbler" was a nineteenth- and early twentieth-century underworld term for a specialized type of criminal who, through combining burglary with a confidence trick, or "sting", acquires a great deal of loot. He shows in exemplary fashion the "dishonour among thieves", for his victim is usually another criminal who has acquired his booty by theft in the first place.

The term "hobbler" comes from "to hobble", in the sense of "to perplex or impede". This can be done physically, but is more often achieved through mental trickery. In Tolkien's world, we often see superior forces "hobbled" by opponents who deploy perplexing riddles or legally binding word games as a replacement for brute force. Despite initial appearances, Bilbo Baggins the Hobbit is an excellent candidate for a "Master Hobbler". Being a Hobbit, there is little opportunity for Bilbo to intimidate physically, so he is more likely to learn how to perplex, impede, and confuse his foes, rather than confront them. If he is to survive, he must quickly learn to use his wits and a few tools of his profession to relieve other criminals of ill-gotten loot.

Bilbo Baggins's technique is perfectly described in criminal-world slang that was first recorded in Britain in 1812 (and has been used ever since): "to hobble a plant" means "to find booty that has been concealed by another; to spring the loot by deception or theft". The phrase means roughly "the finder hobbles the planter". This is the technique Bilbo employs in each major encounter – whether the "planter" (the criminal-cum-victim) is a Troll, Goblin, Gollum, Dragon or

Bilbo Baggins in Rivendell Library during his retirement

Dwarf. In each case, after tricking and evading his opponent, the hero-burglar gets "to spring the loot". And so an ordinary, mild-mannered Hobbit rapidly evolves into a first-class heroic Hobbit hobbler.

We are not quite through. Curiously enough, there are still more ways of linking our Bag End Baggins to the underworld criminals of Victorian Britain. Three are quite notable: to "bag" means to capture, to acquire or to steal; a "baggage man" is an outlaw who carries off the loot or booty; and a "bag man" is the man who collects and distributes money on behalf of others.

What's in a name? In Bilbo Baggins of Bag End we have a borough- and burrow-dwelling bourgeois burgher who, by hiring himself out as a professional burglar, baggage man and bag man, became that most un-Hobbitish of creatures – a hero.

PART
SEVEN

HEROES OF THE THIRD AGE: PART III. HOBBITS AND DÚNEDAIN

THE ONE RING

J R. R. Tolkien once described how the discovery of the ring
in an Orc cavern by Bilbo Baggins was as much of a surprise
to the author as it was to his Hobbit hero. Tolkien knew
as little of its history as Bilbo Baggins did at that time. He also
explained how it grew from a simple vehicle of plot in *The Hobbit*
into a central image of his epic tale *The Lord of the Rings*.

Just how did this ring come to be just lying there in the
caverns of Tolkien's mind? The truth is that Tolkien's ring quest
has its roots in an ancient storytelling tradition that dates back to
the dawn of civilization. The richness of this heritage is evident
in Tolkien's own writing and in his deep understanding of the
ancient wisdom preserved in those myths and legends.

The Lord of the Rings as it was first conceived was to be a
fairy-tale sequel to *The Hobbit*. However, by the second chapter,
Bilbo Baggins has long vanished and his heir, Frodo Baggins, has
inherited Bag End and the ring. The novel begins its shift away
from the fairy-tale world towards an epic world of romance and
myth, as Gandalf the Wizard reveals the true and sinister nature
of the ring, and as Frodo Baggins discovers that he has inherited
an adventure more fantastic than Bilbo's Quest of Erebor. Indeed,
dragon-slaying appears to be a small matter compared with the
challenges that the bearing of the One Ring will soon impose.

Tom Bombadil, a folkloric figure in the traditions and legends of Elves, Dwarves and Men

FRODO BAGGINS AND THE RING

Tolkien's acknowledgement that "names always generate a story in my mind" has revealed a great deal about Hobbits in general, and Bilbo Baggins in particular. What special qualities of character might the name Frodo Baggins have evoked that might contribute to the hero of the Quest of the Ring?

Here we need to observe a linguistic chain of logic: Frodo in original Hobbitish was Froda and, as Tolkien knew well enough, Froda in Old English meant "Wise" while its Norse equivalent,

Frothi, was a name meaning "Wise One". In Old English literature and Scandinavian mythology, the name Frodo (or Froda, Frothi, Frotha) is most often connected with heroes renowned as peacemakers. In the Old English epic *Beowulf* there is Froda, the powerful King of the Heathobards who attempts to make peace between the Danes and the Bards. In Norse mythology there is a King Frothi who rules a realm of peace and prosperity. As we shall see, this is certainly prophetic of Frodo's eventual role as Frodo the Wise and Frodo the Peacemaker in the Quest of the Ring.

And the Baggins surname? What further baggage was passed on along with the Baggins name to Frodo the Ring-bearer? Through our investigation into Bilbo Baggins's heritage as master burglar, we have already sorted out a good deal of the Baggins baggage, especially those pieces applying to various names for specialized and highly skilled forms of larceny. In the context of the One Ring, there is a startling linkage between the name Baggins and another specialized underworld occupation: the "bagger" or "bag thief". A bagger is a thief who specializes in stealing rings by seizing a victim's hand. Remarkably,

A typical Hobbit

the term has nothing to do with baggage, but was simply a homonym derived from the French *bague*, meaning "finger ring". The word appears to have been in common usage between about 1890 and 1940.

It seems that from the beginning the Baggins name contained the seeds of the plots of both *The Hobbit* and *The Lord of the Rings*. For even one step beyond Bilbo's and Frodo's well-advertised and very useful skills as burglars, one might also conclude – from the perspective of the Ring Lord (or, indeed, Gollum) – the Baggins baggers of Bag End were also natural-born ring thieves.

SAMWISE GAMGEE

There is no doubt that Frodo Baggins's companion and servant, the rough-cut working-class Samwise Gamgee, was what Tolkien called a typical "plain unimaginative, parochial" Hobbit. However, Sam's courageous heart and unswerving loyalty to Frodo more than once save the day in their long quest. His deeds also display what Tolkien described as the most unlikely Hobbit characteristic of the "amazing and unexpected heroism of ordinary men 'at a pinch'."

Once again, we discover a Hobbit's name serving as the key to his character. Samwise Gamgee was the son of Hamfast Gamgee. So just as we found that his master's name, Frodo, means "Wise",

Frodo and a Barrow-wight

logically enough, we discover that Samwise, transliterated into Old English, means "Half-wise" or "Simple". Sam's father's name is equally descriptive: Hamfast, again in Old English, means "Home-stay" or "Stay-at-home". Both are unambiguous names for simple garden labourers.

Samwise's family name, Gamgee, is both descriptive and playful. The original Hobbitish name was Galpsi, which through usage, Tolkien tell us, became abbreviated through usage from Galbasi, meaning "from the village of Galabas (Galpsi)", which is itself derived from *galab*, meaning "game", "jest" or "joke" and *bas*, meaning "village" or, in Old English, *wich*. So we have the "Game Village" that translates to English as Gamwich (pronounced "Gammidge") that becomes Gammidgy and ends up with the name Gamgee, meaning "game", "jest" or "joke".

In the half-wise Samwise Gamgee we have the perfect foil to his master, the wise Frodo Baggins. Simple Sam Gamgee is both game for any challenge and, despite terrible hardships, always willing to attempt a jest or joke to keep everyone's spirits up during the Quest of the Ring.

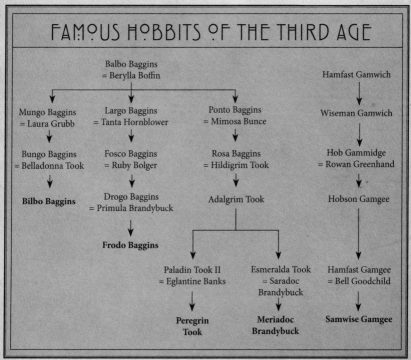

FAMOUS HOBBITS OF THE THIRD AGE

Balbo Baggins
= Berylla Boffin

Hamfast Gamwich

Mungo Baggins
= Laura Grubb

Largo Baggins
= Tanta Hornblower

Ponto Baggins
= Mimosa Bunce

Wiseman Gamwich

Bungo Baggins
= Belladonna Took

Fosco Baggins
= Ruby Bolger

Rosa Baggins
= Hildigrim Took

Hob Gammidge
= Rowan Greenhand

Bilbo Baggins

Drogo Baggins
= Primula Brandybuck

Adalgrim Took

Hobson Gamgee

Frodo Baggins

Paladin Took II
= Eglantine Banks

Esmeralda Took
= Saradoc
Brandybuck

Hamfast Gamgee
= Bell Goodchild

**Peregrin
Took**

**Meriadoc
Brandybuck**

Samwise Gamgee

Next page: Frodo and Sam in the Dead Marshes

GANDALF THE GREY

Gandalf is an amusing and reassuring presence in the opening chapter of *The Lord of the Rings*, in much the same way that an odd and distant uncle entertains everyone with charming firework displays and amateur magician's tricks at a family party. Gandalf's subsequent transformation into a grave and formidable figure comes as something of a surprise for the reader. The force of his personality and his sense of purpose have increased tenfold in this world of high epic and romance as he takes on the guise of the archetypal powerful wizard in the tradition of Merlin.

In *The Silmarillion* and *Unfinished Tales*, Gandalf the Grey is revealed as one of the Istari, an ancient order of wizards ("Istari" means "wizard" and "wizard" means "wise man."). The Istari are a brotherhood who arrive on the western shores of Middle-earth at the end of the first millennium of the Third Age and are in origin Maiar, angelic spirits, sent by Manwë in bodily form to bolster resistance to Sauron.

Only once in *The Lord of the Rings* is Gandalf's origin alluded to and then only obliquely by Treebeard, who mentions that Gandalf and Saruman arrived in Middle-earth some time "after the Great Ships came over the Sea". This is a puzzling statement in that the Ent is likely referring to the ships of the

Númenóreans, whose homeland had long before been destroyed at that point, towards the end of the Second Age.

ISTARI OF VALINOR, WIZARDS OF MIDDLE-EARTH

	NAME IN VALINOR	MAIA OF	KNOWN TO THE ELVES AS	ALSO KNOWN AS	
SARUMAN THE WHITE	Curumo ("the Cunning One")	Aulë	Curunír ("Man of Skill")	Saruman of Many Colours	Sharkey ("Old Man")
GANDALF THE GREY (LATER THE WHITE)	Olórin ("Dream Vision")	Manwë	Mithrandir ("Grey Pilgrim")	Tharkún ("Staff Man") (to the Dwarves)	Incanus ("North Spy") (to the Haradrim)
RADAGAST THE BROWN	Aiwendil ("Bird Friend")	Yavanna	Radagast ("Tender of Beasts")	Radagast ("the Bird Tamer")	Radagast ("the Simple")
THE BLUE WIZARDS	Alatar ("Aftercomer") Pallando ("Far One")	Oromë	Ithryn Luin ("The Blue Wizards")	Morinehtan ("Darkness Slayer") Romestamo ("East Uprising")	???

IN THE NAME OF THE WIZARD

T he name Gandalf originally appears as "Gandalfr", listed in the ancient Old Icelandic "Dvergatal" (Roll of the Dwarves). The Old Norse elements of Gandalfr are either *gand* and *alfr*, or *gandr* and *alf*. The last element of both, *alf/alfr*, means either "elf" or "white". If the first element is *gand*, it suggests magical power. Alternatively, the element *gandr* means an object used by sorcerers, such as an enchanted staff.

As to direct translation of the name Gandalf, there are three fairly solid suggestions: "elf wizard", "white staff" and "white sorcerer". All three translations are admirably suitable names for a wizard. However, Tolkien would likely argue that each translated aspect of this particular wizard had other definitions hidden within. The implications of these played a considerable part in shaping the fate of the character.

The translation "elf wizard" applies descriptively because Gandalf is the wizard most closely associated with the Elves of Middle-earth and the Undying Lands. "White staff" is an apt name as the staff was the primary symbol by which wizards are known. It symbolizes the ancient sceptre of power in disguise (*skeptron* being the Greek word for "staff"). The translation of Gandalf as "white wizard" is initially confusing, as his Grey Elven name was Mithrandir, which means "Grey-wanderer" – an apt name for a grey wizard. However, this conflict in meaning appears to be a foreshadowing of Gandalf the Grey's transfiguration into Gandalf the White.

Gandalf the White

MERLIN AND GANDALF

I n Arthurian romance, Merlin is the greatest of all wizards. He is the future king's mentor, adviser and chief strategist in both peace and war. He is also the presiding intelligence and organizing principle in Camelot. He is its supernatural protector. Merlin is immortal, but has mortal emotions and empathy. He is an enchanter who communes with spirits of woods, mountains

Next page: Gandalf fights the Balrog in Moria

and lakes, and has tested his powers in duels with other wizards and enchantresses.

The parallels with Gandalf are clear. Merlin and Gandalf are both travellers of great learning and have long, white beards; both carry a staff and wear broad-brimmed hats and long robes. They are both non-human beings. And, just as Merlin was the chief counsellor of King Arthur, the future king of a unified Britain, in his court of Camelot, so Gandalf is the mentor of Aragorn II, the future king of the Reunited Kingdom of the Dúnedain. Yet, for all their closeness to power, they have no interest in worldly power themselves.

Although the archetypal figures of hero and wizard are clearly similar in pagan saga, medieval legend and modern fantasy, the context within which they act is clearly different. The moral universe of Christian Arthurian romance is remote indeed from that of the Norse myths and tales of Odin and Sigurd. Curiously, although Tolkien's world is a pagan, pre-religious one, his hero, Aragorn, has strict views on absolute good and evil. Aragorn may be a pagan hero, but he is even more upright and moral than the Christian King Arthur.

ARAGORN THE HERO

F irst encountered by Frodo the Ring-bearer as Strider the Ranger in a public house in Bree, Aragorn is gradually revealed as the ideal warrior king of his age. He is the central figure in a dynastic history that begins over six thousand years before in the annals of Middle-earth's history.

In the figure of Aragorn, J. R. R. Tolkien creates his ideal hero of a mythic age and, in so doing, gives expression and definition to what the cultural anthropologist Joseph Campbell called the "Hero with a Thousand Faces". In his 1949 book of that title, Campbell presented the theory that all mythologies could be understood as parts of one universal myth cycle, which he called the "monomyth".

The monomyth is a single great cycle of tales marking out each stage in the hero's life: from birth to death; then on again, through resurrection and rebirth. Ultimately, all heroes are one hero, and all myths are one myth. The eternal circle or ring resembles a serpent swallowing its own tail/tale – the *ouroboros*.

Of course, Tolkien created Aragorn before Campbell published his monomyth theory, but Tolkien had theories of his own. The reason for Aragorn's resemblance to Campbell's universal hero is that both authors viewed the mythic dimension as a timeless sacred realm of ideal entities and archetypes. This is also why – Tolkien implies – the lives of many of the heroes of Middle-earth are comparable to heroes of what he called the "Primary World", and why the heroes of myths and fairy tales have a resemblance to his archetypal heroes of Middle-earth's "myth time".

This is especially true of Aragorn II, Chieftain of the North Kingdom. He is chosen as the redeeming hero and liberator of Middle-earth. He is known by many names: Aragorn, Estel (Hope), Strider, Telcontar, Longshanks, Thorongil, Elfstone, Isildur's Heir and, ultimately, High King Elessar of the Reunited Kingdom of Gondor and Arnor. Gifted with a lifespan three times that of ordinary men, Aragorn is a hero with the time and ambition to live through virtually every stage in Campbell's monomyth.

King Aragorn II

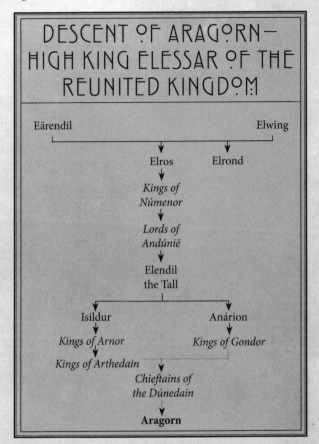

DESCENT OF ARAGORN— HIGH KING ELESSAR OF THE REUNITED KINGDOM

Eärendil — Elwing

Elros   Elrond

Kings of Númenor

Lords of Andúnië

Elendil the Tall

Isildur   Anárion

Kings of Arnor   *Kings of Gondor*

Kings of Arthedain

Chieftains of the Dúnedain

Aragorn

ARAGORN, ARTHUR AND SIGURD

E nglish-language readers of *The Lord of the Rings* frequently register a connection between the legendary King Arthur and Aragorn. What is not often apparent, however, is that twelfth- to fourteenth-century Arthurian romances are often based on fifth-century Germanic-Gothic oral epics – epics that now only survive in the myths of their Norse and Icelandic descendants. Tolkien was far more interested in the early Germanic elements of his tales, which link Aragorn with Sigurd the Völsung, the archetypal hero of the Teutonic ring legend.

Although all three heroic warrior kings – Sigurd, Arthur, Aragorn – are clearly similar, the context out of which each arises – in pagan saga, medieval romance and modern fantasy – is very different. The creation of the essentially medieval King Arthur and his court of Camelot, with its Christian ethos, naturally resulted in some reshaping of many of the fiercer aspects of the early pagan tradition. Sigurd the Völsung is a wild warrior who would have been out of place at Arthur's polite, courtly Round Table. Curiously, although Tolkien's Aragorn is a essentially a pagan hero, he is often even more upright and ethically driven than the Christian King Arthur.

Despite these differences of context, however, the comparison between Arthur, Sigurd and Aragorn demonstrates the power of archetypes, especially in dictating aspects of character in the heroes of legend and myth. If we look at the lives of each of these three, we see certain patterns that are identical: Arthur, Sigurd and Aragorn are all orphaned sons and rightful heirs to kings slain in battle; all are deprived of their inherited kingdoms and are in danger of assassination; all apparently the last of their dynasty, their lineage ending if they are slain; all are raised secretly in foster homes under the protection of a foreign noble who is a distant relative – Arthur is raised in the castle of Sir Ector, Sigurd in the hall of King Hjalprek, and Aragorn in Rivendell in the house of Elrond.

During their fostering – in childhood and as youths – all three heroes achieve feats of strength and skill that mark them for future greatness. They all fall in love with beautiful maidens, but must overcome several seemingly impossible obstacles before they can marry: Arthur to Guinevere, Sigurd to Brynhild, Aragorn to Arwen. And, ultimately, by overcoming these obstacles they win both love and their kingdoms.

ELROND AND THE FELLOWSHIP OF THE RING

Just as Bilbo Baggins found refuge with and guidance from Elrond Half-elven in *The Hobbit*, Tolkien has Frodo Baggins, a generation later, arriving in Rivendell in need of protection and good counsel on a different quest. Not only did this refuge for Elves and Men house a vast library of Elvish lore but, as Tolkien acknowledged in *The Hobbit*, Master Elrond Half-elven was himself a living witness to six thousand years of history and lore. In common with other refuges in fairy tales and myths, there is something about Elrond's Rivendell that attracts questing heroes. This is something best viewed through an examination of its Sindarin name, Imladris.

Imladris, which means "deep cleft dale", refers to its location in a hidden rock cleft at the foot of a pass through the Misty Mountains, an idea repeated in Rivendell's Westron name, Karningul, meaning "cleft valley", as well as, of course, in "Rivendell" itself. The Sindarin Imladris is an Elvish allusion to the Calacirya ("cleft of the valley of light") in the Undying Lands, a mountain pass between Eldamar and the paradise of Valinor during the Years of the Trees.

In ancient Greece, there was another sacred "cleft of light". This was the Oracle at Delphi, which was built in a narrow pass under Mount Parnassus, sacred to the sun god Apollo. Delphi means "cleft" in Greek. The Oracle of Delphi was the "cleft" through which the sacred light of Apollo flowed. Like the light of the Trees of the Valar, Apollo's light was of both a literal and a metaphorical nature, for Apollo the god of the sun was also the god of knowledge and of prophecy. Within the sanctuary of the Temple of Apollo, there was hidden a cleft rock or fissure in the sacred mountain from which rose vapours that induced a prophetic trance. Kings and lords of the ancient world consulted the Oracle at Delphi if they faced a major undertaking such as a war or expedition.

It was no accident that the Fellowship of the Ring was forged in Imladris. Both Imladris and Delphi were houses of consultation that were approached before any great adventure or campaign of war. However, in Middle-earth as well as in ancient Greece, the future was not fixed, but determined by personal courage and will. Delphi and Imladris were both places where fellowships were created and journeys begun.

In *The Lord of the Rings*, the Ringwraiths attempt an attack on Rivendell/Imladris but are rapidly repelled when the Bruinen river floods and sweeps them away. This is comparable to a historical attack made on the sacred sanctuary of Delphi during the Persian Wars (499–449 BCE). As recorded by the Greek historian Herodotus, the Persian King Xerxes (reigned 486–465 BCE), upon invading Greece, commanded his bodyguard to march on the unfortified sanctuary of Delphi. In this attempt, the Persian forces were swept away by a thunderous series of flash floods, followed by a massive crush of landslides that blocked the mountain passes. This attempted violation of the sacred sanctuary of Delphi was followed by a series of astonishing defeats in battle, and an end to a war that for Xerxes was nearly as disastrous as the end of the War of the Ring was for Sauron.

Next page: The Fellowship of the Ring arrive at Rivendell

FRODO BAGGINS
RING-BEARER
Hobbit

GANDALF THE GREY
Wizard

ARAGORN
THE DÚNEDAIN
Man

BOROMIR OF GONDOR
Man

FELLOWSHIP
OF THE RING

SAMWISE GAMGEE
Hobbit

LEGOLAS GREENLEAF
Elf

GIMLI SON OF GLÓIN
Dwarf

MERIADOC BRANDYBUCK
Hobbit

PEREGRIN TOOK
Hobbit

LEGOLAS OF THE WOODLAND REALM

egolas Greenleaf is the sole representative of the Elves in the Fellowship of the Ring. Legolas is the only son of the Elvenking of the Woodland Realm in Mirkwood who appears in *The Hobbit*. In *The Lord of the Rings*, Tolkien reveals the Elvenking's name as Thranduil – meaning "vigorous spring" – while Greenleaf is both Legolas's epithet and the meaning of his name.

Tolkien used the Anglo-Saxon name Mirkwood for the Westron name of this great forest, to convey a sense of superstitious dread, much like that of the haunted forests of ancient German myth and of Brothers Grimm fairy tales. In Middle-earth, this dread of the Mirkwood (and, indeed, forests in general) was shared by Dwarves, Orcs and most races of Men. However, Legolas and all Elves – like the ancient Celtic tribes – saw the great forests very differently: from the inside looking out. The Celts – like Tolkien's Elves – were worshippers of trees, and their great forests were perceived as natural wonders. Wooded valleys and glens were portrayed in their literatures as flooded with golden light by day and brimming with moonlight and starlight by night. In the forests were found miraculous herbs and medicine, as well as nourishing foods.

The forests, for Tolkien's Elves and the Celts alike, provided all

Woodland Elf

the materials needed for life – from the making of clothing to the building of homes. And so it was usually deep in dense woods, by caves, wells or fountains, that Tolkien's Elves – again like the ancient Celts – revered the spirits of wood and water and found their sacred places and oracles.

GIMLI AND THE DOORS OF MORIA

Entry into the kingdom of the Dwarves in *The Hobbit* is by way of a secret door in the mountain of Erebor. The magic door is a common theme in fairy tales, from "Ali Baba" to "The Pied Piper", and Tolkien repeats it in *The Lord of the Rings* when the Fellowship of the Ring arrives at the west door of the Dwarven underground city of Moria (Khazad-dûm). The door is sealed shut but, as Gandalf tells the company, "these doors are probably governed by words".

Creatively speaking, words are the key to all of Tolkien's kingdoms of Middle-earth, a world he explored and discovered through language, runes, gnomic script and riddles. Words unlocked the doors of Tolkien's imagination. In this case, the west door of Moria is unlocked and opened by uttering the Elvish word *mellon*, meaning "friend". This secret password to enter Moria must have sounded somewhat ironic to the sole Dwarf member of the Fellowship of the Ring. For it was Gimli the Dwarf's ancestor King Durin III who in the Second Age sealed the door shut against Sauron the Dark Lord, and a second direct ancestor, King Durin IV, who in the Third Age was slain by the Balrog who drove the Dwarves out of Moria.

King Durin IV is also Tolkien's means of linking the magic rings of myth and fairy tale to his own tale of the Rings of Power. For it was Durin IV who received the first of the Seven Dwarf Rings, which was believed to be the source of his kingdom's fabulous wealth with its power "to breed gold". The Seven Dwarf Rings have a likely source of inspiration in the dwarfs and rings of ancient German and Norse mythology. In the Norse *Völsunga* saga, one such magical gold ring was known as Andvarinaut, meaning "the ring of Andvari the Dwarf". It was also called "Andvari's Loom" because of its power "to breed gold" and was the ultimate source of the cursed gold of the Nibelung and Völsung treasures.

As Tolkien would have been aware, these ancient ring legends were also the source of the riddling fairy-story "Rumpelstiltskin", which substitutes a spinning wheel for the dwarf-forged, gold-producing ring.

Gimli the Dwarf

GALADRIEL: THE LADY OF LOTHLÓRIEN

In the mythology of the ancient Welsh, the most enchanting spirits of the forests were the White Ladies, who, in nearly all ways, resemble Galadriel. The White Ladies of the Welsh share the affinity of Elves with starlight. All love to walk through the forest beneath the starlit sky. Like Tolkien's Elves, they were also generally perceived by mortals as having eyes like stars and bodies that shimmer with light. These ancient Celtic forest and water nymphs were guardians of sacred fountains, wells and grottoes hidden in deep forest vales.

To reach these refuges it was commonly necessary to pass through or across water that was – as is said of crossing over a river into Lothlórien – "like crossing a bridge in time". The White Ladies live in a realm outside time and often dwelt in crystal palaces hidden beneath water or floating in air, all glowing with silver and golden light.

In *The Lord of the Rings*, the fairest and most mysterious Elf-kingdom remaining in Middle-earth is hidden within the enchanted forest of Lothlórien ("land of blossoms dreaming"), also known as Lórien ("dreamland") and Laurelindórinan ("valley of the singing gold"). While it seems to have pre-existed it, it is heir to, and to some extent, re-creates the forest kingdom of Doriath in Beleriand, one of whose lords, Amdír, became its

Opposite: The Mirror of Galadriel

king in the Second Age. Its rulers in the Third Age, the Noldorin Lady Galadriel, and the Sindarin Lord Celeborn, are in many ways the archetypal faerie queen and king. "Tall and beautiful, with the hair of deepest gold", Galadriel is robed in white and has great powers of prophecy.

Galadriel's association with water seems deliberate. Wood and water nymphs with supernatural gifts or weapons have a pedigree older than recorded history. In Greek mythology, the Nereid, or sea nymph, Thetis was the mother of Achilles and armed that great hero for battle in the Trojan War. And, in Arthurian tradition, Vivien, the Lady of the Lake, dressed in white and, rising from her palace beneath the water, presented the sword and scabbard of Excalibur to the rightful king. Vivien also raised Lancelot du Lac, before sending him into the world with the arms of war. Such supernatural figures gave protection, inspiration and strength to their protégés, and these characteristics are shared by Galadriel, who presides over a realm of dreams and desires, visions and illusions, gifts and blessings.

ARWEN EVENSTAR AND SNOW WHITE

Many of Tolkien's heroic tales are presented as the histories of "true myths" that in our world have been reduced to the most basic and obvious of fairy tales. He particularly liked to demonstrate to his readers how the tellers and writers of fairy tales often got their stories wrong.

In Galadriel's Lothlórien, for example, we see virtually every element of the story of Snow White: an enchanted forest, a beautiful dark-haired princess (Arwen), a queen with a magic mirror (Galadriel) and a Prince Charming (Aragorn), her long-parted lover to whom she plights her troth in Lothlórien (they meet for the first time and fall in love in Rivendell). Except, as Tolkien suggests, the fairy-tale version of "Snow White" got it all wrong: Galadriel the Queen is Snow White's guardian and protector (and actually her grandmother), not her persecutor; the enchanted forest is a place of refuge and healing; and the

Arwen Evenstar

magic mirror a combination of an oracle and a wishing well.

The Half-elven princess, also known as Arwen Undómiel (the epithet meaning "Evenstar"), is comparable to Snow White in that both are dark-haired beauties with luminous white skin. Tolkien quite pointedly links Arwen to Varda Elentári, the Valarian "Queen of the Stars" who is also known by the epithet Fanuilos, or "Snow White". Tolkien also makes another obvious nod to the fairy tale, in a running debate between Éomer of Rohan and Gimli the Dwarf over the relative beauty of Arwen of Gondor and Galadriel of Lothlórien. So, Tolkien implies, it is easy to see how some mischievous teller of fairy tales might invent a story of a jealous queen asking her magic mirror: "Who is the fairest of them all?"

ELVEN AND MAIAR BLOODLINES OF ARAGORN AND ARWEN

MAIAR	SINDAR	NOLDOR	VANYAR	TELERI
Melian the Maia	Elwë Singolo "Greymantle"	Finwë	Indis	Olwë

Melian the Maia ——— Elwë Singolo "Greymantle"

↓

Lúthien

Dior

Elwing

Elros

- - - - - → Aragorn

Finwë

Fingolfin

Turgon

Idril

Eärendil

Elrond

Arwen

Indis

Finarfin

Galadriel

Celebrían ←

Olwë

Eärwen

WARRIOR KINGS AND ANCESTRAL SWORDS

—·—·◆▶ ◀◆·—·—

The significance of the ancestral sword of the warrior king is a motif of many European myths and legends. King Arthur, for example, is famous for his winning of the Sword in the Stone (sometimes identified with Excalibur). This is an act that duplicates the contest in the *Völsunga* saga where Sigurd's father, Sigmund, alone can draw the sword Balmung that Odin has driven into Branstock, the living "roof-tree" in the Hall of the Völsungs.

Neither Sigurd himself nor Aragorn of the Dúnedain, however, are presented with such contests: they are both given their swords as heirlooms. Their problem is instead that both swords are broken, and neither may use them to reclaim their kingdoms until they are reforged. In Sigurd's case, the sword was broken by Odin in his father Sigmund's last battle, while Aragorn's sword was broken by his ancestor Elendil in his last battle with Sauron. Like the swords of Sigurd and Aragorn, Arthur's sword is supposedly unbreakable; however, through special circumstances, all three are broken.

Once Sigurd has reforged his sword Gram, he sets out at once to reclaim his heritage. He does this by avenging his father's death and reclaiming his kingdom by conquest, slaying the dragon Fafnir and taking the monster's treasure and ring. Sigurd then goes on to win his beloved valkyrie princess Brynhild. To some degree, Aragorn's life mirrors Sigurd's. Once Aragorn's sword Andúril is reforged, he sets off to reclaim his heritage. He avenges his father's death, reclaims his kingdom by conquest, and, after the destruction of the One Ring, wins his beloved princess, Arwen Evenstar.

The nature of Aragorn's sword owes something to both Arthurian and Völsung traditions. Aragorn's sword was

originally named "Narsil", meaning "red and white flame". It was forged by Telchar, the greatest of all the Dwarf-smiths of the First Age. Narsil is broken by Elendil in a battle with Sauron the Ring Lord and is reforged in Rivendell by the Elves of Celebrimbor, the greatest of all the Elf-smiths of the Second Age. Renamed Andúril, meaning "flame of the west", its blade flickers with a living red flame in sunlight and a white flame in moonlight.

In the Völsung tradition, the sword that Odin drives into Branstock and is then claimed by Sigmund is forged in Alfheim by the hero known to the Saxons as Wayland the Smith. The sword has no formal name until it is reforged for Sigurd by the dwarf-like Regin the Smith. The sword is then named Gram, and its blade is distinguished not only for its unbreakability, but also the blue flames that play along its razor edges.

The tale of King Arthur differs from Sigurd and Aragorn in that he does not have his broken sword reforged. Arthur is instead given a new sword, Excalibur, by the enchantress Vivien, who is also known as the Lady of the Lake. As another boon, Excalibur has a jewelled scabbard that will not allow Arthur to be wounded. The blade of Arthur's Excalibur also flickers with a living flame and, like Gram and Andúril, can cleave through iron and stone, yet maintain its razor-sharp edge.

Meanwhile, in Galadriel, the Queen of the Golden Wood, we have a comparable figure to Arthur's benefactor, Vivien. It is Arwen's guardian grandmother who gives Aragorn a jewelled

Opposite: Éomer, Third Marshal of the Riddermark

sheath that makes the sword blade of Andúril unstainable and unbreakable. This is the ancestral sword by which he claims his kingdom and wins the hand of Arwen Evenstar.

BOROMIR AND ROLAND

Tolkien's account of the heroic death of Boromir, the eldest son of Denethor II, the Ruling Steward of Gondor, is redolent of "La Chanson de Roland" (The Song of Roland). Set down at some point in the eleventh century, this is the most famous of the medieval *chansons de geste* ("songs of heroic deeds") and tells the story of Charlemagne's paladin Roland, as he makes his heroic last stand in the Roncevaux Pass in the Pyrenees while under attack by the Saracens. Ambushed and vastly outnumbered, Roland fights valiantly on until his sword breaks and he is overwhelmed by the infidel hordes. As he dies, Roland blows his horn Oliphant to warn Charlemagne of the proximity of his foes. As Charlemagne approaches, the Saracens flee and Roland is able to speak a few last words before he dies.

Albeit on a smaller scale, this battle is comparable to the last stand of Boromir, Gondor's greatest warrior, on the cliff pass above the Rauros Falls on the river Anduin. Ambushed by a troop of Orcs and heavily armed Uruks, Boromir blows the Great

Boromir

Horn of Gondor. Aragorn, like Charlemagne, rushes to the site of the battle, but is too late to help. Boromir utters a few last words before he expires, admitting his guilt in trying to force Frodo to surrender the One Ring to him. While Roland is an ideal Christian hero, Boromir has a fatal flaw, and is driven to near-madness by his desire for power.

Next page: Boromir's funeral boat passes over the falls of Rauros

Boromir has inherited his one-thousand-year-old silver-tipped Great Horn from his Steward ancestor, Vorondil the Huntsman. It is made from the horn of a gigantic wild white ox called the Kine of Araw, which is modelled on the historic aurochs, the now-extinct wild white oxen hunted by the ancient Germans and valued for their horns. By no coincidence at all, Araw is another name for the Valarian huntsman Oromë (meaning "hornblower"), who in turn was undoubtedly inspired by the Welsh god Arawn the Huntsman.

TREEBEARD AND THE ENTS

Among J. R. R. Tolkien's most original and eccentric heroes is Treebeard the Ent, the fourteen-foot-tall "Shepherd of Trees". Treebeard, or Fangorn (to use his Elvish name), resembles something between an evergreen tree and a man. The name Ent came from the Anglo-Saxon word *enta*, meaning "giant", while the portrayal of Ents and their wilder cousins, the Huorns, were inspired by Tolkien's extensive knowledge of the lore and traditions of the Green Man.

Years after the publication of *The Lord of the Rings*, Tolkien acknowledged in an interview that the eccentric characterization of Treebeard was specifically meant as a good-humoured lampooning of his friend and colleague C. S. Lewis (1898–1963), the author of *The Chronicles of Narnia*, complete with his booming voice, his absurd "Hrum, Hoom" interjections, and reputation as an utter know-it-all, who, irritatingly, usually did know it all.

On another level – but also one in which Tolkien took some personal amusement – the Ents were also meant to gently satirize Oxford dons, especially the hidebound philologists (among whom Tolkien would have numbered himself). Like those academics, Ents "were long on the discussion of problems, but slow to take action": in Oxford as in Entwood, action proved unnecessary as the debates often outlasted the problems.

A discussion in Entish, however, would have been a philology student's nightmare. The Ents' language is slow beyond human endurance because each thing named must include the whole history of the thing – "leaf to root" as the Ents might say. Consequently, Ent gatherings, or "Entmoots", with their qualifications, additions, exceptions and verbal footnotes on every point, would have had a special savour for those who were familiar (as Tolkien was) with the editorial meetings of the compilers of the *Oxford English Dictionary*.

Next page: Treebeard and the Ents

MERRY, PIPPIN AND THE DESTRUCTION OF ISENGARD

I t is the Hobbits Meriadoc (Merry) Brandybuck's and Peregrin (Pippin) Took's chance encounter with Treebeard the Ent in Fangorn Forest that ultimately provokes the attack on Saruman's fortress of Isengard, changing the course of the War of the Ring. Both Hobbits are from aristocratic families: Merry is heir to the Master of Buckland and Pippin is heir to the Thain (military leader) of the Shire.

Tolkien gave both Hobbits names that were prophetic of both their temperaments and their roles as courageous (if diminutive) knights errant and members of the Fellowship of the Ring. Meriadoc is a genuine ancient Celtic name, borne by the historical founder of the Celtic kingdom of Brittany, as well as by one of the knights at King Arthur's court. Peregrin's nickname is the name of the father of Charlemagne and the founder of the Carolingian dynasty, Pepin the Short (Pippin in German).

For his part in the slaying of the Witch-king of Angmar, Meriadoc Brandybuck became known as Meriadoc the Magnificent. However, Tolkien informs us, the names Meriadoc and Merry are translations of the original Hobbitish "Kalimac" and "Kali", meaning "jolly". While Merry as a name is a variant of "Mercy", in origin it derives from the Old English *myrige*, meaning "pleasant". However, in a curious and somewhat comical twist, this ultimately appears to originate in the Proto-Germanic *murgjaz*, meaning "short".

Peregrin Took – eventually to become Peregrin I, thirty-second Thain of the Shire – has a given name derived from the Latin *pelegrinus*, meaning "foreign" or "abroad", and related to the Old French *pelegrin*, meaning "wanderer", the Middle English *peleguin*, meaning "traveller" and the modern English "pilgrim" and "to peregrinate". This seems quite an appropriate name for one engaged in a ring quest. And, by an even more curious coincidence, the Old French name for the peregrine – a small hunting falcon – is *hobet* (Anglo-Saxon: *hobby*).

Meriadoc Brandybuck and Peregrin Took

GANDALF: THE WHITE RIDER

A
s we have seen, one way of translating the name Gandalf is as an Old Norse construct meaning "White Wizard", a name that seems unsuited to Mithrandir, the "Grey Wanderer". However, as we have come to appreciate, the hidden meaning of names often predicts the fate of Tolkien's characters.

One might compare the riddle of Gandalf's name to that of Saruman, the original White Wizard. An alternate translation for Saruman's name is an Old English construct meaning "Man of Pain" – a reasonable prediction of Saruman's transfiguration as the evil sorcerer of Isengard. This is the reverse of Gandalf the Grey's transfiguration as Gandalf the White. Once again, Tolkien is acting the part of a magician and has set us up for a conjurer's trick with language: a little verbal manipulation wherein white becomes black, and grey becomes white.

It seems that Tolkien might have been inspired to make one more link between his two wizards' fates through contemplating a couple of alternative translations of the first element in Gandalf's name: *gandr* as "an enchanted crystal" and *gand* as "astral travelling". Remarkably enough, we find that Saruman's downfall comes through his misuse of an enchanted crystal called a Palantír, while the salvation of Gandalf comes through a form of "astral travelling" that permits his resurrection after falling with the Balrog from the Bridge of Moria.

As Gandalf the White, the Wizard offers no explanation for his resurrection. He simply says: "I strayed out of thought and time." It is, perhaps, the best definition possible for "astral travelling" or possibly for that mysterious thing we can now know as the "power of Gand".

In this respect, Gandalf is comparable to the Norse god Odin who, in his shamanic wizard form, travelled between the world of men and the worlds of spirits, and even into the land of the dead. Certainly, Tolkien had this in mind when he gave Gandalf's horse the name Shadowfax, meaning "silver-grey". This is comparable to Grani, meaning "the grey", the silver-grey steed of Odin's champion Sigurd in the *Völsunga* saga. Like Shadowfax, Grani understands human speech. Furthermore, Shadowfax is the offspring of the supernatural horse Nahar, the Valarian steed of Oromë the Hunter; while Grani is the offspring of the supernatural eight-legged horse Sleipnir, which Odin rode through the Nine Worlds.

Next page: Samwise wounds Shelob

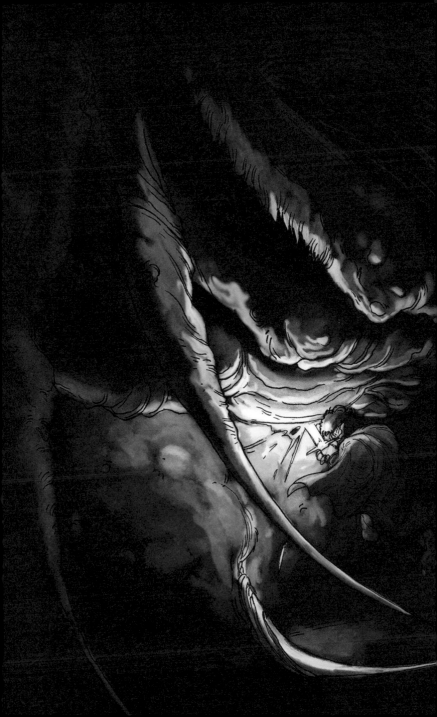

SAMWISE AND SHELOB THE GREAT

I n a personal letter in 1956, Tolkien wrote that a good part of his characterization of his fictional Samwise Gamgee was derived from his experience as a signals officer in the First World War. "My Samwise is indeed … largely a reflexion of the English soldier – grafted on the village-boys of early days, the memory of the privates and my batmen that I knew in the 1914 War."

Batmen were soldiers who were essentially manservants to officers. In the First World War, British officers were from the upper middle classes, or – like Tolkien – were university-educated men; while working-class men were recruited as privates and could ascend only to the rank of sergeant. Sam was a humble, uneducated gardener and employee of the master of Bag End.

The relationship between Frodo and Samwise is very much that of an Edwardian master and servant. Although not uncritical of the class structure and customs of that time, Tolkien was enough of an Edwardian himself to believe that within these roles a bond of mutual respect and loyalty was possible and could be an ennobling thing.

John Garth, the author of *Tolkien and the Great War*, has observed that as the quest progresses, the master–servant relationship largely becomes inverted: "[Frodo] presents the problems, Sam the solutions." In the First World War, he adds, "this process was far from atypical". It was a view that Tolkien observed and recognized: his batmen, he admitted, often proved "so far superior to myself".

One of the most courageous acts in the entire Quest of the Ring is Sam's ferocious defence of his master from the unspeakable horror of Shelob the Great Spider in the Ephel Dúath mountains of Mordor. And, certainly, without the fierce and unquestioning soldier's loyalty of Samwise Gamgee, the wounded and weakened Frodo Baggins could never have crossed the no-man's-land of Mordor to reach the fires of Mount Doom.

KING OF THE GOLDEN HALL

W hen Gandalf rides towards Rohan's royal city of Edoras, Tolkien describes the distant sight of the gold roof of the Golden Hall of Meduseld glinting in the sunlight. The name Meduseld is a modernized version of the Anglo-Saxon for "mead hall". The description of the hall is almost identical to that of Heorot, the Golden Hall of King Hrothgar in *Beowulf*. As Beowulf approaches the kingdom of Hrothgar, the poet catches sight of Heorot's roof gables covered with hammered gold that glistens and glints in the light of the sun.

The Golden Hall of Meduseld

Both of these great halls have even greater, divine models. Meduseld has its divine model in Valinor in the Great Hall of Oromë the Horseman, and Heorot has the Great Hall of Valhalla. This was the "Hall of Slain Heroes", roofed with golden shields. It was the mead hall and heaven of fallen warriors, created for them in Asgard by Odin.

The name of the King of the Golden Hall is Théoden, son of Thengel, and the seventeenth king of Rohan. His name is Anglo-Saxon for "lord" or "king", and is related to Old Norse for "leader of the people" or "king"; in Tolkien's invented language of Rohirric, his name is Tûrac, again meaning "king".

Kingship is important to the world of Middle-earth. To all its peoples, monarchy is the natural political condition and kings are not like ordinary men. This is an old tradition in English thought, and Tolkien was a thorough royalist in his sympathies. Shakespeare wrote in *Hamlet* about how "divinity doth hedge a king". In Tolkien's writing, even when a king goes utterly bad, as with the Witch-king of Angmar, he retains his kingly quality and powers of leadership.

Although a king may become old and weak, like Théoden, his royal gift remains, and, as Tolkien reveals in the episodes that follow, he can shake off his enfeeblement and resume strength and command. (Incidentally, readers of George MacDonald's classic children's fantasy novel *The Princess and Curdie* [1883] will see a certain debt to the story there of the old king, long kept in a sort of stupor by his wicked servants.) And so, with Gandalf's aid, the old king's powers are revived and he once again becomes "Tûrac Ednew", or "Théoden the Renewed", the Lord of the Éothéod, the "Horse People".

Next page: King Théoden leads the Rohirrim into battle

HELM'S DEEP AND THE GLITTERING CAVES

I n the Battle of the Hornburg, Gimli the Dwarf is forced to take refuge and defend the redoubt in the caverns of Helm's Deep. In so doing, Tolkien has the Dwarf discover the Glittering Caves of Aglarond. The writer acknowledged that these caves were in good part inspired by the spectacular real-world caves of the Cheddar Gorge in Somerset.

Legolas, Gimli and Aragorn at Helm's Deep

However, Gimli's vivid descriptions of Aglarond (meaning "glittering caves") make it clear that the Dwarf believes these caves to be the greatest interlocking network of caverns and grottos in all of Middle-earth – a discovery that makes it a potential paradise for Dwarves. Here, once again, Tolkien's precise use of language is worth noting, in this instance the relationship between the word "glittering" and the name Gimli.

Tolkien took all but one of his Dwarves from the "Dvergatal", an Old Norse list of Dwarf names. That one exception is Gimli. This is a name mentioned in a very different Norse text, an ancient poem, part of the *Prose Edda* entitled "Völuspá", or "The Seeress's Prophecy". Gimli, however, is not the name of a dwarf or man, but rather a place. Gimli actually means "glittering" and it is the name given to the Norse paradise: a great golden-roofed hall and kingdom that appears after the great battle of Ragnarök and the destruction of the Nine Worlds.

Just as Gimli was revealed in the wake of Ragnarök as a glittering paradise for the Norse people, so in the wake of the War of the Ring Tolkien has Gimli create a new paradise for Dwarves by colonizing the Glittering Caves of Aglarond.

THE PATHS OF THE DEAD

ccording to Sir James Frazer's influential study *The Golden Bough* (1890–1915), ancient human societies had a king for a year only. Chosen or self-presented in the spring, he was crowned, feted and given everything he could be provided with. And then, late in the autumn, he was killed, so that his blood would fertilize the soil, to "return" the following spring as the new sacred king. "The king is dead, long live the king" is a very old saying. It was to bring back such sacred kings that ancient goddesses made their descents into the underworld.

Frazer's ideas were highly influential for much of the twentieth century and are discernible in the story of Aragorn, who, before he comes to Minas Tirith to be acknowledged as king of Gondor, must pass through a form of the underworld in his journey along the Paths of the Dead. When Aragorn emerges, it is as the king of the Dead Men of Dunharrow, in command of a terrifying army of undead warriors against the Corsairs of Umbar. Like Jesus in the New Testament – for Frazer, an example of the sacred king – Aragorn descends into "hell" to free the "imprisoned spirits" of the dead.

Aragorn's claim as the true heir to the Dúnedain Kingdom is confirmed by his "healing hands", and he is marked apart by his Elvish knowledge of the healing properties of plants and herbs.

After the Siege of Gondor, Aragorn uses the herb Athelas to bring Éowyn, the Shieldmaiden of Rohan, back from the death-like trance induced by the Black Breath of the Witch-king. In Carolingian legends, Charlemagne was reputed to have been able to cure those struck down by the plague, the "Black Death", by using the herb known as sowthistle. In both cases, these herbs worked their magical cures only if administered by the healing hands of the king. This is acknowledged in the folklore of Middle-earth, where, Tolkien tells us, the common name for Athelas is Kingsfoil.

THE SHIELDMAIDEN ÉOWYN

In the Battle of Pelennor Fields, the Witch-king of Angmar is slain by Éowyn, the Shieldmaiden of Rohan, and by the Hobbit Meriadoc Brandybuck. Éowyn belongs to an ancient tradition of warrior women in the world of epic romance and saga. In the Norse *Völsunga* saga and the German *Nibelungenlied*, we have comparable heroines in the twin figures of Brynhild and Brunhild. In the *Völsunga* saga, Brynhild is a valkyrie, a beautiful battle maiden who defies Odin and is subsequently pierced with a sleep-thorn and imprisoned within a ring of fire. Like the Sleeping Beauty, she is awakened from sleep by a hero – in this instance, Sigurd the dragon-slayer, with whom she falls in love.

Éowyn slays the steed of the Witch-king

In the *Nibelungenlied*, Brunhild ("armoured warrior maid") is the
warrior-queen of Iceland who falls for Sigurd's medieval German
equivalent, Siegfried.

Both Brynhild and Brunhild are based on the historic
and notorious Visigoth Queen Brunhilda. Just as there are
elements of Brynhild/Brunhild to be found in Éowyn, so

there are comparisons to be drawn between Sigurd/Siegfried and Aragorn. Likewise, it is Brynhild/Brunhild's hopeless love for Sigurd/Siegfried that Tolkien draws on for Éowyn's own unrequited feelings for Aragorn. Siegfried, for example, is betrothed to another queen, Kriemheld, in the same way that Aragorn is betrothed to Arwen Evenstar. And, just as the Warrior Queen Brunhild is transformed by marriage into the wife of King Gunnar, so too is Éowyn the Shieldmaiden, through her marriage to Faramir, the brother of Boromir and son of Denethor II, the Steward of Gondor, though without the tragic consequences.

BLACK SAILS AND THE SIEGE OF GONDOR

At the Battle of the Pelennor Fields during the Siege of Gondor, there is one episode that mirrors the climax of the ancient myth of the Greek hero Theseus. In the Greek tale, the hero is revealed as the heir to the throne of Athens. His father welcomes him back – despite prophecies of regicide. When Theseus discovers that Athens must pay an annual tribute of seven youths and seven maidens to King Minos of Crete as sacrificial victims, he decides to end this bloody payment. Theseus sets out in a black-sailed tribute ship to Crete where, along with other Athenians, he is to be sacrificed to the bull-headed Minotaur in the Labyrinth of King Minos.

On his departure, Theseus promises his father, the king of Athens, that, if he slays the Minotaur and releases his people from bondage, he will change the sails to white for his return voyage as a signal of victory. In the rush of his triumph, however, Theseus forgets his promise. Tragically, his father, the old king, sees the tribute ship returning with its great black sail still set. Believing his son Theseus to be dead, and his nation still enslaved, the old king throws himself from the high lookout prow of the Acropolis onto the rocks far below.

In *The Lord of the Rings*, we have Denethor, the Ruling Steward of Gondor, who sees a mighty fleet of the black-sailed ships of the Corsairs of Umbar sailing up the river Anduin at a critical moment in the Battle of the Pelennor Fields. Believing his son Faramir is dying of a poison wound, and all his forces upon the battlefield are being overwhelmed and slaughtered, the Steward assumes that the enemy reinforcements in the black-sailed ships will make the defence of Gondor impossible. Mad with despair, Denethor reads the signs wrongly and commits suicide by burning himself to death on a pyre; however, like Theseus's father, the Steward of Gondor is tragically mistaken. Like Theseus, Aragorn has in fact been victorious and has captured the black-sailed ships of the Corsairs. This proves to be a turning point in the battle and the war.

Just as Athens is freed from the threat of the tyrant and Theseus succeeds his father as king, so Gondor is freed from the threat of the Witch-king, and Aragorn is restored as the king.

BATTLE AT THE BLACK GATE

O f all the stories of medieval German epic and romance, the tale of Dietrich von Bern's war with Janibas the Necromancer is the most redolent of Aragorn's war with Sauron the Ring Lord and his servants. Certainly, there are many aspects of this tale that are suggestive of the major themes and characters in Tolkien's War of the Ring.

Dietrich von Bern was based on a real historical figure: Theodoric the Great (454–526), king of the Ostrogoths, who later became ruler of Italy. However, in his fictional cycle of tales, his rise to power is not unlike that of Tolkien's Aragorn.

Dietrich's foe, Janibas the Necromancer, is a powerful wizard who reveals himself in the form of a phantom Black Rider on a phantom steed who commands massive armies of giants, evil men, monsters, demons and hell-hounds. In the high mountains of the Alps, Dietrich discovers that Janibas has laid siege to the castle of the beautiful Ice Queen of Jeraspunt.

The Necromancer's hordes surge like a black sea at the gates of the castle. In a valiant attempt to raise the siege, Dietrich slaughters all before him, but this proves futile because, at the Necromancer's signal, the dead rise up to fight again. However, upon discovering that Janibas commands his forces by means of an iron tablet, Dietrich pursues the Black Horseman himself. Striking Janibas down from his phantom steed, Dietrich lifts his sword and smashes the iron tablet. As the tablet breaks, the glaciers of the mountains split and shatter, thundering down in massive avalanches that bury the whole evil host of giants and phantoms and undead forever.

The legend of Janibas as the Black Horseman is like a combination of Sauron and the Witch-king of Angmar, leader of the Ringwraiths. The iron tablet is comparable to Tolkien's One Ring, and the climax of the tale reads very much like the ultimate battle at the Black Gate of Mordor. The result of the destruction of the iron tablet on Janibas's evil legions is identical to that of the destruction of the One Ring on Sauron's legions and the end of his kingdom of Mordor.

THE REUNITED KINGDOM AND THE HOLY ROMAN EMPIRE

Tolkien often pointed out how many readers saw the connection between Aragorn and King Arthur, and yet missed the connection between Aragorn and Charlemagne.

It seemed to Tolkien that, in his task of reconstructing the Reunited Kingdom of the Dúnedain from the ruins of the ancient kingdoms of Arnor and Gondor, Aragorn was historically comparable to Charlemagne, who reconstructed the Holy Roman Empire from the ruins of the ancient provinces of the classical Roman Empire. Both Aragorn and Charlemagne fought many battles that resulted in the expulsion of invaders and the formation of military and civil alliances that brought about an era of peace and prosperity.

Once their foes were defeated, both Aragorn and Charlemagne quickly re-established the ancient common laws, set up a common currency, rebuilt the ancient roads and re-established postal systems. Both inspired a golden age of culture, art and literature. Charlemagne became essentially the first Holy Roman Emperor (in all but name: he was actually crowned as "Emperor of the Romans") while Aragorn was renamed Elessar Telcontar and crowned High King of the Reunited Kingdom.

Geographically, Tolkien saw in the Reunited Kingdom an expanse of lands akin to the expanse of Charlemagne's empire. The action of *The Lord of the Rings* takes place in the north-west of Middle-earth, in a region roughly equivalent to the European landmass. And indeed in a letter Tolkien remarked: "The progress of the tale ends in what is … like the re-establishment of an effective Holy Roman Empire with its seat in Rome."

FRODO THE PEACEMAKER

I n ancient literature and myth, variations on Frodo's name are linked with the role of "peacemakers". In *Beowulf*, there is Froda the King of the Heathobards, and in Norse mythology King Frothi rules over a realm of peace and prosperity. Also, in Icelandic texts, we find the expression "Frotha-frith", meaning "Frothi's peace", referring to a legendary "age of peace and wealth". This is in tune with Frodo's compassion and attempts to avoid bloodshed in all his adventures. After the carnage of the war, Frodo the Wise becomes a respected counsellor and peacemaker throughout Middle-earth.

Certainly, within the Shire, Hobbits experience the equivalent of the Norse legend of Frotha-frith with Frodo's Peace, the year after the Battle of Bywater, in the time of the First Blossoming of the Golden Tree of Hobbiton. The war-ravaged Shire is transformed and filled with Elvish enchantment. In that year, many children born to Hobbits are golden-haired and beautiful, and everything prospers in the Shire. This is the Great Year of Plenty that marks the beginning of a golden age of the Shire, the Age of Peace and Wealth. Yet, as he ages and continues to suffer from a lingering wound that will not heal, Frodo the Wise's concerns pass beyond the affairs of the mortal world.

Like his namesake Froda the Heathobard, Frodo Baggins

passes from the sphere of the mortal world into the immortal realm of fairy tale and myth. Frodo the Ring-bearer has, through his heroism and suffering, achieved the status of the saviour of Middle-earth in Myth Time. Just as Tolkien's earlier hero Eärendil the Mariner and the Saxon hero Eärendel the Bright Angel are meant to be mythic forerunners like the historic prophet John the Baptist, so Tolkien's Hobbit hero Frodo the Ring-bearer and the Saxon hero Frothi the Peacemaker are suggestive of that other historic and biblical Prince of Peace.

LAST SAILINGS: AVALON AND AVALLÓNË

Tolkien modelled the bittersweet ending of *The Lord of the Rings* – the departure of the Ring-bearers from the Grey Havens – on the myths and legends surrounding King Arthur's departure to the isle of Avalon. It is an ending that is derived from the Celtic side of the Arthurian tradition, rather than the Teutonic one. After his final battle, the mortally wounded Arthur is taken on a mysterious ship by three beautiful faerie queens. The ship carries the wounded king westward across the water to the faerie land of Avalon, where Arthur is healed and given immortal life.

This end to Arthur's mortal life is very like the end of Tolkien's novel. However, it is important to point out that this is not Aragorn's end – Aragorn remains to die within the mortal world. The supreme reward of this voyage into the land of the immortals is reserved for another. The "wounded king" who sails on the Elf Queen Galadriel's ship across the Great Sea towards the Elven towers of Avallónë on Tol Eressëa is Frodo the Hobbit Ring-bearer, who is rightly the real hero of *The Lord of the Rings*.

Curiously, throughout *The Lord of the Rings* and *The Hobbit*, although the Hobbits appear often to be a comic foil to the larger heroic personalities of the Men and Elves, nearly all the greatest deeds are achieved, or are instigated, by Hobbits. Bilbo's adventures result in the death of Smaug the Dragon and the discovery of the One Ring. It is Meriadoc Brandybuck and Peregrin Took whose mission among the Ents results in the destruction of Isengard and the downfall of Saruman; while Meriadoc's bravery on the Pelennor Fields results in the slaying of the Witch-king of Angmar. It is Samwise Gamgee who wounds and blinds Shelob the Great Spider, and, most important of all, it is Frodo who brings the One Ring to the Crack of Doom, where its destruction results in the downfall of Sauron the Ring Lord and the end of the War of the Ring.

In the end, the Hobbits are the real heroes. It is the humble Frodo Baggins who achieves the Quest of the Ring. He does so at the cost of his health and a poisoned wound that will not heal. The wounded Hobbit – like the wounded Arthur – is taken over the water. It is not Aragorn the King, but Frodo – the hero of the heart – who is chosen to sail to the land of the immortals.

Frodo sails from the Grey Havens

Next page: Haunted Barrow-downs

INDEX

PAGE NUMBERS IN ITALIC TYPE REFER
TO ILLUSTRATIONS AND CAPTIONS